The End of Fear

Download the soundtrack at
wenzlmcgowen.com

I lay in my bed, unsure whether I was dreaming. My dreams had become almost indistinguishable from reality. The only difference was that in my dreams, I could walk through walls, and most people couldn't see me. I thought, *Maybe ghosts are people stuck between the dream world and the real world.* I played around with these kinds of thoughts, somewhat amused by my imagination, until Jeff offered me a job.

Jeff was my cellmate. I wasn't sure what crime he had committed or why he was in prison. Even though he was my cellmate, I had never talked to him, but I knew his face well. He normally had a serious and focused look in his eyes, but when I met him in my dream, he flashed me a smile.

It was one of those strange dreams in which I would get up and float right through the closed door. Jeff was on the other side of the door, standing in the middle of the hallway, and prisoners and guards were walking through him. He appeared slightly transparent, but I could still see his expression. He was smiling. He had a very professional smile, the kind you see when someone offers you a job that they really want you to take.

He said, "Hello, Greg. Would you like to make fifteen grand a month?"

"Is this a dream?"

"No, I'm serious."

"Yeah, you are serious, but this is still my dream, right?"

"No, it's not just *your* dream. I'm here too, but I don't have time for a philosophical debate with you. I would like to offer you a job."

I did not say anything, so he continued. "It's not a typical job, but you would be perfect for it."

Guards and prisoners were walking past, but none of them seemed capable of seeing or hearing us. Jeff said, "The thing about this job is that you have to work at a mental hospital. I did it for several years before I began helping to recruit people from the prison system."

"Wait, you work here?"

"Yes. I am not a criminal. I help prisoners do something meaningful with their lives. Would you like to work for the military?"

"What? How? What is this?" I was confused and not sure if I should take this imaginary conversation seriously.

Jeff sensed my confusion and said, "Look, I know this might seem a bit odd to you, but please give me a few moments of your attention and then decide for yourself." His voice was calm and reassuring, "You would be working for an organization called PsyOp. We focus on a unique approach to strategic defense. The only downside is that you would have to be diagnosed with a mental illness that requires you to regularly visit a mental hospital. There will be a bed for you, and that's where you will spend most of your time. You will park your body there while you go to work. You have an incredibly strong imagination, and you have a very powerful intention. You are barely using any of your gifts at this point. We can train you and show you how to make use of your gifts."

"You mean I would work through my dreams, or whatever this in-between reality is?"

"Yes. You see, this is not just your imagination. It also intersects with reality. You can do real work from here. Let me show you."

Jeff glided through the wall into another cell, and I followed him. Then he hovered over a prisoner who was sitting on a bed.

4

Jeff looked at me and said, "He can't see or hear me, but my intention can influence him, especially if I am very focused. You see the newspaper over there on the floor? I will try to make him pick it up."

He pointed to the prisoner who sat below him. "I will merge with his body and then imagine picking up the paper. My intention field will interfere with his intention field."

He merged with the prisoner's body, and after some time, the man slowly reached between his feet and picked up the newspaper.

Jeff separated again and said, "He will not have noticed any inconsistencies in his reality. Most people never question where their thoughts come from."

We floated back into the hallway, and he asked, "What do you think about fifteen grand a month? That's not a bad offer, right?"

"Hmm, 15K a month is a lot of money. That's almost 200K a year. But something about manipulating others doesn't feel right."

"You're not manipulating others; you're helping them in a particular way, helping a part of them. And don't forget, we can also get you out of prison right away. Once you're out, you'll work two weeks on and two weeks off."

"But I have to work from a mental hospital?"

"Absolutely."

"Why?"

"To protect PsyOp. No one can know about this kind of work, and no one will believe a mental patient."

"Damn, this is pretty crazy."

"Yeah, it's very exciting work. It gives the military a lot of new opportunities. Think about what we can accomplish with this ability. Anyway, I'll be switching cells tomorrow. I need to look at a few more potential employees. Here's what you need to do if you

5

decide to take the job. This coming Wednesday, before you go to sleep, visualize my face and say my name. You should be able to find me."

CHAPTER 2

The next day, Jeff was gone, and I got a new cellmate. If my experience with Jeff wasn't a dream, then I had two days before I was supposed to see him again. I still wasn't sure if I should take the job, but it was a fuckton of money, and my life was in ruins anyway.

Before I got arrested, I had been living on a subway platform in New York City. I used to spend my time begging for money and chugging beer. Steel Reserve was my favorite, strong and cheap. I used to drink them with my friend Joey, before he tried to kill himself.

He used to say, "It is easier to be dead than to live on the street." I didn't think he was really going to do it, but one day he jumped in front of the subway. Miraculously, he survived. Six months later, he was back on the streets in a wheelchair, but he was smiling like he was at his sister's wedding. His long blond hair was clean and tied back in a ponytail, and his blue eyes glowed with excitement. I was happy to see him; I thought we were going to drink a six-pack or something. Instead, he tried to teach me how to meditate. He kept telling me that meditation would make my life much better.

One time, I was sitting on the L-train platform at the 8th Avenue station, and Joey was next to me in his wheelchair. He was telling me how meditation had helped him deal with the pain of his injury. He was so excited, he could not stop talking about it.

With an animated voice and wild gesticulations, he insisted, "Meditation is straightforward. You cross your legs, keep your back straight, and focus on your breath. If a thought comes in, just let it pass and return your focus to your breath."

He said that if I kept repeating this exercise, it would change the way I saw the world.

I certainly did not like the world I saw. My ass was on the cold floor, and everyone else was standing there in fancy shoes. Some of the businessmen had shiny leather shoes they'd probably just gotten polished by an underpaid immigrant.

Joey kept going. "If you practice meditation for a couple of months, you'll realize that your true home is in your heart. You can never be homeless if you're in control of your breathing; it will always bring you back to your true home."

I told him to go shoot an infomercial. His enthusiasm was getting on my nerves. But when he finally gave up and left me alone, he had me almost convinced. At any rate, I was willing to give it a try.

I sat there on the subway platform and did what he had told me to do. I was trying to be mindful, but after a few hours, my back and legs started to hurt. Keeping my attention on breathing became extremely difficult, but I fought through the pain. In the end, though, the physical discomfort did not bother me as much as the emotional pain I began to experience. Sitting still seemed to bring up things I was trying to forget.

Suddenly, I remembered how my parents had died. I could see them smiling when they got into their car for the last time. My heart was beating fast and hard, and my fists were clenched. Joey had told me not to react to emotions or thoughts, so I tried to focus, but I was hyperventilating. Images were flashing in front of my eyes, and I was powerless to stop them.

I tried as hard as I could to focus on my breath, but the pictures in my head made it very hard to stay calm. I could feel my frantic breaths smacking my upper lip like a whip. I saw my parents' blood dripping

8

from the wreckage of the crumpled car, but this time I saw it from a different perspective. Everything seemed slightly transparent. I could see both of them floating above the vehicle. They turned into brightly glowing orbs and then disappeared.

Joey's voice wrenched me back to reality. "Yo, you've been sitting here for three hours without moving. I didn't want to disturb you, but I brought you some food."

He handed me a cardboard box. I could see green leaves protruding from it, and I thought, *What the hell is this? We never used to eat like this.*

Joey explained that he had gone to the farmers market and bought some local organic vegetables for me. He said that when you face the shit inside your chest, your body changes. It needs better nutrition to rewire itself. So I pulled out big pieces of green leaves and started chewing them. They tasted like shit, but Joey told me that I would get used to it.

He was looking directly at me. I saw the eyelashes above his blue eyes, and there was a moment I'll never forget. Joey was sitting in his wheelchair. People were behind him, and they were part of it too. The whole thing—reality, I mean—just kind of stopped. People still moved, but there was a break, like someone had rolled up the screen and said, "Okay, the movie is over."

Joey smiled and said nothing. I could tell that he was there too, experiencing the break, and I suddenly wondered, *But who is he and who am I?* I could not come up with an answer, and that gave me a strange feeling. When Joey left, that feeling grew into a giant monster. I could almost see its teeth. But its attitude was just straight up nasty.

The thing demanded that I know the answers. It asked, "What was that moment you just had? Who do

9

you think you are? What are you doing with your life?"
And it was right—I had not thought about these things
for a while. I could feel a knot in my chest, and I
wanted to get some beer.

I realized that beer was something else I had not
thought about for a while. I didn't know how long it
had been. Time had gotten pretty blurry. But now
everything seemed urgent. I got up quickly and hurried
to the corner store.

I could feel an evil grin floating in midair. It
wasn't speaking to me, but I could feel its thoughts.
Good, get some beer. That will keep you safe.

I hadn't been protecting myself. I was just sitting
on a subway platform with my eyes closed. What had I
been thinking? I felt like I'd woken up from a dream, or
maybe I had fallen back into one. What the hell had
happened? Was Joey fucking with my head? I mean, he
had just made me eat a box of green leaves.

It felt good to be back in the store. Looking at
the beer selection was one of my favorite things to do. I
always chose Steel Reserve, but the fact that I had so
many choices was simply amazing. That's why I loved
America.

I gulped down the beer, the can still inside a
brown paper bag, and I stayed close to the store in case
I wanted another one. I ended up drinking three more.

I was stumbling down the street that night when
I ran into my old friend Caroline. She was always
hanging around lower Manhattan. At least that was
usually where I saw her. She was beautiful, but I could
not afford her anymore.

One summer, when I still had some money left
from my parents, I spent it all on her. We got close, but
when I ran out of money our relationship meant nothing
to her. That added another layer of filth to the rotten
feeling in my chest. Just thinking about her made me

angry. I thought, *Everyone is full of shit, but they smile at you when you have money in your pocket.*

I raged in my head about what a foul place this world can be. It disgusted me, and I wanted to punch someone in the face. Then I heard a voice. "Yes, that's right . . ."

I saw the outline of a dark figure hovering above me. I was sitting on the sidewalk, and this fucking disgusting thing was floating there. It smelled bad, too—or maybe that was the trashcan next to me—but it certainly was not good. Was I going crazy?

"Yes, you certainly are," the voice whispered in my ear. "You are a drunk fool wasting your life in this foul place."

And I thought it was right, so I nodded in agreement. The feeling in my chest grew even nastier, and it felt like an oil rig was drilling deep into my heart. I was losing strength, and I could see a dark cloud spreading around me.

I woke up in the same spot the next morning. The trashcan stood beside me, and the sun was shining on my crusty lips. Joey sat next to me.

"What the fuck happened to you?" he asked. I looked at him, but it was not the same anymore. His smile seemed fake, and I almost told him to shove his happiness up his ass. Instead, I just looked away.

"Hey, what's going on?" he asked.

"Joey, I can't do this anymore."

"Do what?"

"That meditation bullshit. It's not for me." I wanted to jump down his throat, but I just told him politely to leave me alone.

The next couple of days were horrible. I got into a fistfight with a stranger, and when the cops came, I punched one of the officers in the face. Before I realized what was happening, they had me on the ground in handcuffs.

At first, being in jail wasn't that bad, but after my talk with Jeff, there was now another layer to it. I thought a lot about what it might mean to go insane. I wasn't sure if it was crazy to take Jeff's offer seriously, but at the same time, I felt like it wasn't just a dream. While my thoughts twirled in circles, I became angry at Joey again. That meditation shit had really messed up my mind, or maybe my mind was already messed up to begin with. Either way, things were messy, and reality was no longer easily defined.

CHAPTER 3

Wednesday arrived, and I was curious to see how consistent my dream reality was. I decided to try to meet Jeff.

I lay in bed and focused on my breathing. After some time–I don't remember how long it was—I visualized Jeff's face and repeated his name. I imagined talking to him.

Suddenly, my body started to shake. I heard a popping sound and felt a strong pulling sensation, as if I were falling down an elevator shaft. My vision became blurry, and I saw swirling, shimmering colors. Then everything came to a sudden halt. I found myself standing in front of Jeff. We were on a tropical beach. The sun reflected off the ocean, and tall palm trees moved in the breeze.

I was extremely surprised, and so startled that I did not know what to say. I looked at Jeff, probably with my mouth hanging open, but I remained silent.

Then he said, "Did you get a chance to think about it? Do you want to work for PsyOp?"

I wasn't sure what to say. I hadn't really thought about whether I should take the job or not. I couldn't seriously consider his proposition without feeling like I was losing my mind, but Jeff was looking at me with a serious expression. He wanted an answer.

Jeff was still slightly transparent, but he seemed genuine, at least in the sense that he really wanted me to work for him. I thought about what to say.

Then Jeff said, "Would you rather spend your time in this prison or make fifteen thousand a month defending your country? Even if you get released, you'll just go back to living on the streets. You're wasting your talent, Greg. Do something with your life! Join us and get to know how reality really works. I know it all seems confusing now, but we will give you proper training and answer all your questions. You can be a pioneer, working with cutting edge technology and doing things most people can't even imagine. You *can* imagine them, Greg. That's why you're here. You have a gift. Use your gift."

Although he still looked serious, he had made me smile. He was right. I was wasting my life. A highly paid position in a secret organization did sound exciting. I thought about it for a moment longer and said, "Yes, I have decided. I will work for you."

"Good choice. We'll need you to commit to at least a year. But if you sign a two-year contract, we can offer you a little more money. You'll still start out at 15,000 a month, and if you're doing a good job, we'll raise your salary to 20,000 a month after the first six months. But we are flexible; you can also wait six months to sign the two-year contract."

"Okay, maybe I'll sign the one-year contract for now and see how it goes," I replied.

"All right, but before we get into specifics, let me explain a few more things. We only want you to be using these skills when you're working for us. Don't do any visualization exercises when you're not working. We'll also give you meds that will help you go right to sleep. When you're at the hospital, you'll still get meds, but those will be slightly different. In fact, they'll do the opposite; they'll help you to leave your body more efficiently.

"Also, once we get you diagnosed, you will be legally required by your contract to take the medication. When your contract with us ends, we'll do our best to erase the memories, and most likely you'll believe that you were just crazy. You'll just be glad that you've gotten out of the hospital. Sounds good?"

"Sounds intense, but at this point, it's probably my best option," I said. "I guess I'll do whatever is required."

"Perfect," Jeff replied. "The quickest way to get diagnosed with a mental illness is to attack another prisoner and then scream something crazy, like "I'm Jesus!" or something. Think you can manage that?"

"Man . . . fuck . . . *this* is crazy . . . but I guess I can do it."

"Great. Do that during lunch tomorrow, and we'll work on getting you transferred."

I still had some doubts, so I said, "You guarantee that I'll get out of the hospital after my contract ends?"

"Yeah, PsyOp is a professional organization. We treat our employees well and never disappoint anyone."

"I guess I have to take your word for it."

"Seriously, don't worry about that. Right now, let's talk a little more about the kind of work we do. Sometimes you will work around the clock while your body is sleeping the whole time. Also, I forgot to mention that you'll get a chip implanted in your forehead. It's tiny, so you'll never notice it. The chip measures fluctuations in the energy field your body produces. It alerts PsyOp when you leave your body and when you return. The part of you that is here talking to me on this wonderful beach is a coherent quantum field. A quantum field occurs when several superposition particles have a coherent vibrational pattern. Our scientists discovered this fact decades before the public heard anything about it, so we've been able to build quite spectacular things in this domain. The chip is one of them. The chip will be installed at the hospital, and your body will absorb it after a year. Only one surgery is necessary, and it's not even surgery; it's like getting a tattoo. Sound good?"

"Eh . . . I guess . . ." *Not really*, I thought. But then I thought about the money and shrugged it off.

"We need the chip for security," Jeff explained. "We need to make sure that our workers only leave their bodies when they're working for us."

"But what if people accidentally leave their bodies?"

"That's why we have the chip. You will be monitored."

"I see."

"Okay, let's get the contract signed."

Jeff was wearing something that looked like a watch. He pressed some buttons, and a green hologram that looked like a file drawer full of folders appeared between us.

"How is this possible?" I asked. "How can your watch create this? How can you bring something like this with you when you leave your body?"

"You're also wearing clothes, right? Everything produces a quantum field. We built this technology in the physical dimension before we figured out how to take it into the nonphysical. You'll be surprised what consciousness can do."

Jeff reached into the cabinet and pulled out a folder. He opened it and showed me a form that pretty much reiterated what we had just talked about, but in complex legalese. I entered all the required info, including my bank account number.

"You can use your index finger to sign," Jeff said.

I signed the contract.

"Okay, my friend. It was a pleasure doing business with you. Don't forget to cause a scene during lunch. Remember, you are Jesus!"

"Oh, yeah . . . right."

"You remember how to get back? Just visualize your body and align with it." Then Jeff disappeared.

CHAPTER 4

The next day, I woke up with a bad taste in my mouth
and a tight feeling in my chest. I was embarking on a
treacherous path, but I was determined to follow
through with it.

My skin felt sweaty, and my hands were
trembling when I walked to the cafeteria. Without
thinking about it, I ran towards an inmate and punched
him dead in the face. It was a good punch, and he fell to
the floor.

I began screaming, "I am Jesus! I am Jesus!" I
was immediately tackled by a guard and quickly
handcuffed. I continued screaming, "You can crucify
me, but you cannot take my eternal soul!" I didn't have
to say those words, and they surprised me when they
came out. I guess I was in character.

The next vivid memory I have of that event is
the big metallic doors and neon-lit corridors of Kings
County Hospital. Zombie-like creatures wandered
aimlessly through the halls. I saw a young man banging
his head against a closed door while nurses and doctors
passed by without comment. They were people, but
something about them felt even colder than the floor in
the subway. A prison guard escorted me to a door.
When he opened it, my eyes met those of a psychiatrist,
and I instantly felt misunderstood. His face was glazed
over with a layer of icy indifference. I began to feel like
I had voluntarily stepped into a nightmare. Doubts crept
into my mind.

The psychiatrist asked me to take a seat. My
hands were still cuffed, and the guard who had brought
me to the room stood beside me, his hands folded in
front of him.

Was I going insane? Was Jeff even real? I
realized that the answers to these questions weren't

going to change my situation—especially if I told the psychiatrist that an invisible person in another reality had offered me a job. I realized it didn't matter anymore anyway. I had done something completely crazy, and I began to question my own sanity. Maybe I *would* be safer in a mental hospital. This thought calmed me down a little, and I answered the psychiatrist's questions as honestly as I could.

He asked me about my family, and I told him that my parents had died. He said, "I am sorry to hear that. I hope you don't mind me asking, but what was your relationship like?"

"It was Okay. They died when I was quite young. I loved them very much."

"Was there any abuse or mental illness in your family?"

"No, not that I know of," I answered. "I only have positive memories of them."

As I said that, I began thinking about my mom's smile and sadness flooded my heart. She used to bring me to school, and at home, we sang songs together. Sometimes we sat on the porch and watched the deer grazing in our backyard.

My dad used to build paper airplanes with me. He had a special way of folding the tip that made them fly slower and longer. But I wasn't going to talk about that. It hurt too much just thinking about them.

The psychiatrist was looking at me expectantly, but I said nothing. At that point, I felt like I had the choice to either break down crying or pretend that it was the psychiatrist's fault, so I raised my voice and said, "Who cares! Why do my parents matter? They're fucking dead!"

The psychiatrist scribbled something on his notepad. Then he said, "Do you believe you are Jesus?"

"No!" I yelled.

He wrote some more and then asked, "So why did you cause a scene in the cafeteria? Why did you attack another prisoner, saying you were Jesus?"

I had no other answer, so I shared the truth. "Jeff said that I had to do that in order to work for the military!"

"Who is Jeff, and where did you meet him?"

"Jeff recruits people from the prison system. I met him on a beach . . ." I began to see how crazy I sounded.

"Where was this beach?"

"I don't know."

"Well, how did you get there?"

"I visualized Jeff's face, and I suddenly landed on the beach."

"Interesting . . .," the psychiatrist mumbled to himself as he continued scribbling on his pad. "Hearing voices . . . intrusive visions . . . reality breaks . . . imaginary interactions . . ."

After a while he looked up, and in an indifferent voice he said, "You have schizophrenia. But don't worry, there is a treatment that will at least suppress the symptoms. I will prescribe you Zyprexa. You'll take it once a day, probably for the rest of your life."

I looked around. The guard was still standing there, staring blankly into the distance. The severity of my situation started to sink in. I was now locked in a mental hospital, diagnosed with a mental illness. A part of me hoped that Jeff would keep his promise, but another part was hoping that I would be cured of my mental illness.

A nurse entered the room, gave me a blue jumpsuit, and told me to change in the bathroom. The guard took off my handcuffs. I shook my hands, stood up, and walked to the bathroom. I took off my old clothes and put on the blue jumpsuit. I looked in the mirror and stared into my own worried eyes. "What have I done?"

The nurse and the guard escorted me to my new room. There was a bed on the left and another in the far-right corner that was already occupied. My new roommate appeared to be sleeping. His sheets were pulled over his head, and only a little bit of his hair was visible. It was blond and reminded me of Joey's.

On the desk beside my bed was a red book with a four-word title written in white: *Access in Ten Minutes*. I lay down and opened the book.

It was full of symbols I did not understand. There was text too, but my rational brain did not decipher the meaning. I realized quickly that understanding the text was not the point. If I wanted to get through this book in ten minutes, I only had enough time to look at each line once. As soon as I began reading like that, it seemed like some other part of my mind started processing the information. I still did not understand anything, but something in my brain reacted to it. I heard crackling sounds, like a computer installing new software.

I shut my eyes and saw green lines forming a grid. The grid started pulsing in and out to the rhythm of my heart, creating a dimension of depth in both directions. My body started tingling, as if thousands of tiny roots were growing through my tissues. I was terrified, but I could not stop the process. As the sensation continued, my resistance subsided, and I found myself feeling cold and indifferent.

Suddenly, a new image appeared in my field of vision. It was a black screen with red letters that read, "Welcome Agent 496," and below that, "Start Training."

I heard a voice say, "To enter, focus on *Access*." I did as the voice instructed and heard more crackling sounds, this time accompanied by moving lights. Then I materialized into what looked like a classroom.

There was a teacher standing in front of a holographic blackboard and maybe thirty other students sitting in chairs——or loosely floating above them, actually.

I drifted into a chair and felt as if a magnetic force was keeping me in position. The teacher looked at me and said, "You must be Agent 496. Welcome to Psy 101."

I saw a guy with blond hair a few rows in front of me. He looked like Joey, but I couldn't see his face.

A few more people floated into the classroom, and the teacher greeted each one. Their numbers were 497, 498, 499, and 500. Then he said, "Most of you are new to PsyOp. You probably have many questions. I will do my best to answer as many as possible, but this is a very fast-paced program. I will cover only as much as is necessary. PsyOp deals with the layered information networks, or the multiple dimensions of the universe. There is a way things work, and there is a way people believe they work. PsyOp focuses on making use of the way things work while maintaining a public belief that supports the economy, which is crucial for the well-being of all.

"The economy functions through self-interest, or selfishness. If we all try to maximize our personal profit, we end up benefiting everyone. But this isn't an economics class; you should have learned those things in high school. Here, we focus on only one piece of the puzzle: fear.

"There needs to be a healthy amount of fear within society, because fear is what fuels selfishness. You need to be afraid that you won't get enough; that way, you'll perpetually strive to get more. However, a new emotional trend has begun to disrupt the very core of our system. I say an emotional trend because often people aren't even aware that this shift has occurred. It is, simply put, that they prefer to give rather than take.

This sounds nice, I know, but it is a threat in disguise. Too much positive emotion threatens the structure of our economy. It's very simple. A system built on selfishness needs to be maintained by selfishness, and in order to keep selfishness as the driving emotion of our economy, a certain level of fear needs to be maintained.

"What we do is identify friction points and resolve them. Friction is created by individuals who challenge beneficial beliefs and spread new beliefs to others. It doesn't matter if they are true or not; we are not concerned with telling the public the truth. That wouldn't be good for the economy. We need to make sure that people try to get as much as possible in this one life, even if that means that we have to turn them against each other.

"Once we identify problematic people, we use two strategies to divert their energy. First, we try to get them to work for us. Second, we block them. The first strategy targets the selfish tendencies of an individual. We do not need to recruit them to make them allies. They don't even need to know about us. All we have to do is water their selfish tendencies. So even if they do come up with radical ideas that could endanger our economy, by fostering their selfishness, we turn them into contributors. If a person seeks power and wealth, they immediately benefit the economy. Even if they come up with a new philosophy and a new business model, we foster selfishness until that new model is compromised and corporatized. Let's take some time to look at Strategy One in more detail.

"If someone begins to discover universal truths, they can be influenced easily and tempted to compromise their realizations in order to gratify their ego. Everyone wants to be the hero of the story, so we help them become the hero. We feed that part of themselves. This allows us to bend the truth so it can be woven beautifully into the control system we are building.

"If this first strategy fails, we switch to the second strategy. Strategy Two focuses on blocking the energy of someone who attempts to break out of the control system. This can be done by applying Strategy One to the individual's social environment.

"For example, if a scientist discovers something about this universe that would negatively affect the market, then we feed the selfish tendencies of their colleagues, friends, and family members. We manipulate their actions to make the scientist look crazy or to cause the scientist to lose all credibility. Then we can foster thoughts within the scientist that suggest he or she is, in fact, crazy. If their entire social circle doubts them, it's easy to make them doubt themselves. Sometimes they even check themselves into a mental hospital, and we can again apply Strategy One.

"We give them experiences like all of you have had. We allow them to walk into their imagination, where we meet them and offer them a job. Even if they refuse the offer, this experience pushes them deeper into self-doubt and fear, which produces the conditions we consider mental illness. But mental illness can be a good thing, especially if it affects people who could threaten the growth of the economy.

"Strategies One and Two can be used skillfully in any number of combinations. You can get quite creative in this field. Any questions?"

A young man raised his hand, and as he did so, an electronic voice announced, "Agent 491 has a question."

He said, "This sounds very unethical to me. Are there any boundaries?"

"Yes, there are boundaries in this field. You will only work within the preexisting tendencies of a human being. This means you are always helping one part of them. People have self-destructive tendencies, and helping them fulfill these purposes is not evil, because it is the will of a tendency within them. Does that make sense?"

"I guess . . ."

"You don't sound very convinced. If this work is not for you, you don't have to work for us. But you know the consequences. It's your choice."

"Okay, it makes sense. You help certain parts of people."

"That's right, but not just any parts: the good parts, the parts that make the economy work. Sometimes it might seem a little unethical, but you'll quickly see that not everyone can do whatever they want; there needs to be order within society. We are doing good work, but we have a lot of responsibility, and sometimes we have to make tough choices.

"You know the famous ethical dilemma involving train tracks? You are standing on a bridge and below you is a train track that splits into two separate tracks. One person is tied to one of the tracks, and five people are tied to the other. If you don't do anything, the train will kill the group of five people, but if you switch the lever, the train will be directed to the other track and kill only one person. By switching the lever, it may seem like you have killed one person—and you have— but really you have saved five. In the same way, we make hard choices in this work, but those choices create order. In turn, that order allows the economy to function, which allows many people to live comfortable lives.

"I know many of you were homeless and have lost your families. If the economy had been better, you would have had a job. If the medical industry had been better, perhaps your families could have been saved. So really, you are the saviors who will work towards those goals, and if we build a system that is totally under control, we can make everyone's lives better. Any questions?"

The room was silent. Suddenly the electronic voice announced, "Agent 491 is experiencing strong emotions."

The teacher said, "491, please stand up."

When 491 stood up, he turned around for a second. I was shocked. It was Joey. His blue eyes were radiant, and there was a slight smile on his face.

The teacher said, "You are polluting the atmosphere in this classroom. Emotional vibrations are very perceptible here. We cannot work with you like this. Either you quit now, or we will have to adjust your vibration artificially. In other words, you either spend an indefinite amount of time in the mental hospital or allow us to adjust your vibration."

"Okay," Joey said, "adjust my vibration."

A translucent spiral appeared and surrounded Joey. Thin lines of electricity seemed to be traveling between him and the spiral while his body was shaking violently, but his facial expression did not change. He looked completely relaxed. Suddenly, there was a loud pop and a flash of white light. Joey transformed into a glowing ball of light. The teacher was knocked back against the wall, and then a second flash enveloped the entire room.

I couldn't see anything. I seemed to be floating in an infinite ocean of white light, but this was not ordinary light. It rippled through the core of my being and filled me with unimaginable joy and love. Time seemed to have stopped. It seemed that I was not even human anymore. I was in an infinite moment, and I was just a pure expression of unconditional love.

I noticed shapes that began to emerge in this new, ethereal reality. I could see my parents floating towards me. At first, they looked like glowing orbs, but when they got closer to me, they began showing some physical properties. They embraced me with gentle smiles, and it felt like we merged and became one within an intricate web of vaporized love.

At that moment, it felt like I had everything I could ever want and knew everything I could ever know. I tried to stay with them, but they said it was not yet my time. We started to drift towards a darker spot, and I realized that I came out of a ball of light. It was so beautiful and wise; it seemed to be a visual representation of an energy that could not be expressed with words.

We drifted toward a tunnel, and I suddenly felt a strong pull. I landed back in my body, wakening with tears running down my cheeks. I felt happy beyond words, and I started to laugh uncontrollably. Then I realized that my roommate was sitting up in his bed, tears also running down his cheeks, and like me, he laughed uncontrollably. Joey looked at me and said, "Isn't it the most beautiful thing ever?"

At first, I was speechless, and then I burst out with, "What? How did you get here? What did you do?"

He laughed and said, "I surrendered to the divine. Infinite power comes through surrender. PsyOp only knows the power of control; they don't know the power of surrender. I had to show you what is beyond. You might not see this body again, but hey, it is just a body. That experience you had is eternal; it will always be with you. Never fear death, or anything else for that matter. Good luck, my friend."

A nurse came into the room and said, "Joey, the psychiatrist wants to see you."

He got up and walked out of the room. His legs must have healed.

CHAPTER 5

I got a new roommate. I found out later that his name was Adrian. We didn't talk at first, but we looked at each other for a second. He had dark skin and dark hair. There was a determined look in his eyes that stirred up an uncomfortable feeling of familiarity in me, like he was an old friend who wasn't going to let me get away with the lies I was telling myself. I looked away and closed my eyes.

I tried to sleep, but the black image reappeared behind my eyelids. The red words flashed, "The networks are down." Each time I closed my eyes I saw that image, like I was looking at a computer screen in my head. I began to wonder if the image would stay in my head for the rest of my life, or if they would uninstall the software when my contract ended.

Then I began thinking about Joey. What he did was pretty insane. Who knew what they would do with him? I guess he did jump in front of a train and survived. How had Joey gotten like that? He literally blew the minds of the whole class. I wondered if the teacher had the same experience. That would be crazy. He probably couldn't teach this shit anymore if he did.

My new roommate sat up and asked, "The networks are down?"

"Yeah, I guess."

"What happened?"

I told him about my experience, and he listened to every word I had to say. I asked him how long he had been with the organization, and he said, "A year, but I have to retake this bullshit class. I like doing my own thing, you know? They don't like that."

We talked a little bit, and it turned out that he used to be homeless and had lost both of his parents too.

Then I tried to go to sleep again, but the flashing image still kept me up. I tried imagining something else, but it was all I could see when I closed my eyes.

I remembered the meditation technique that Joey had taught me, and I began to focus on my breathing. After an hour or so, I realized that I was no longer fixated on the flashing image. I could feel a warm sensation and a joyful tickling in my chest. I began to imagine a white light within me. I couldn't see the light, but I could feel it. I focused all my attention on how this light made me feel and imagined it spreading throughout my body.

After a long time, the flashing image disappeared, and the text changed to the words *Start training*. I focused on the link and said *Access* in my mind.

I landed back in the classroom. The old teacher was gone. His replacement was wearing a black suit. He seemed to be in his late fifties, and he looked like he wanted to retire. A sluggishness appeared in his eyes. They moved slowly, and although he welcomed every student that arrived, he didn't seem to mean it. I could hear the hesitation in his voice.

After students filled every seat, the teacher said, "My name is Erick Dolster. Call me Mr. Dolster if you like. I understand you almost finished Psy 101. Do all of you understand Strategies One and Two?" He paused and then said, "Okay, does anyone have questions about the strategies?"

I was listening with one ear, but most of my attention was focused on the joy within me. I still felt the tingling in my chest.

Suddenly, the electronic voice announced, "Agent 496 is feeling heightened emotions."

Mr. Dolster looked at me and told me to stand up. I obeyed, and he asked, "May I adjust your frequency?"

I hesitated for a moment, but then I said, "Okay."

The spiral came from the ceiling and wrapped itself around me. Electrical impulses began shaking my body. I tried to think about what Joey had said, but the current was too intense. I couldn't relax.

I started to feel the same pain in my chest that I used to feel when I lived in the subway. Self-doubt began flooding my mind, and I was afraid. The fear rippled through my body. Then a wave of anger and hatred washed over me, followed by a wave of jealousy. I was feeling jealous of Joey.

The current stopped, and the teacher said, "Much better, much better. Sit back down."

I felt empty and indifferent. The pain in my chest was gone, but it left behind a void. There was nothing left to think about because I didn't care about anything. At the same time, though, I felt alert and compliant.

The teacher said, "It is essential that we all stay within the same spectrum of vibration. We have to work as a team. We will give you Vibrometers, which you can take with you on your missions. When you or your partner enter a raised vibratory field, we can help each other stay within the safe frequency range. This is the essence of our work. We help society stay within a workable frequency range.

"You might ask what these frequencies are. They are probability distributions on the subatomic level, a resonance pattern of potential futures that we experience as emotions. When someone experiences a certain type of emotion, they're likely to take certain types of actions. We're interested in maintaining emotions or probabilistic resonance patterns within the range of self-serving actions.

"To maintain a healthy economy, we need people to be motivated by self-interest, and self-interest is based on the fear of scarcity, or any type of fear, actually. Fear is our anchor point, and from there we can build many beneficial social networks. So let's start with some practical examples.

"The CEO of ClarCo, which is an agriculture company, got off track. His vibration had to be adjusted. The problem was that he got carried away by Eastern philosophy and began to rethink the purpose of the company. He began to question the very foundation of capitalism and to work on reconfiguring the company. He had the idea to teach Eastern philosophy to his workers, while giving them more responsibility and freedom. He began to implement a new power dynamic called the advice model.

"The advice model gives each worker executive control. All they are required to do is ask a specialist and someone affected by their decision. So any worker can make investments or change the business in any way. At the same time, he taught the workers how to meditate and do yoga, which raised their vibrations drastically. As a result, this company became a huge problem for us. The employees all began to operate outside of the predictable spectrum, and selfishness no longer guided their actions.

"It might sound like a good thing, but it added too many variables, and we could no longer predict the future of the company. If you have unpredictable components within a complex system, it can potentially destabilize the whole system. We had to engage and change the trajectory of the company. The plan was to apply Strategies One and Two at the same time. We had ten agents monitoring the CEO around the clock, and after we had collected enough data about his personality, we decided to destabilize his personal life, while simultaneously creating resistance within the company.

"We fostered jealousy in his colleagues and set him up with beautiful women to tempt him into cheating on his wife. After his life came crashing down, we planted thoughts of suicide in his head. He ended up seeing one of our psychiatrists, who then prescribed him medications to stabilize his vibration.

"Just to make sure that he would not raise his vibration again, we also played with his dreams. Dreams are also intention sensitive. With the help of focus aligners, we gave him nightmares about the philosophies he cherished. The stress and fear he experienced forced his psyche to revert to a more predictable mode of operation. He eventually abandoned his lofty goals, and the company returned to the standard capitalist model.

"This example is one we are very proud of. However, in recent times we have experienced more resistance. The source of the resistance is unknown, and we have not found effective ways of dealing with it. It seems that the overall vibration of human consciousness has been rising due to glowing orbs that radiate at a very high frequency. Their origin and their interest in humanity are unknown to us, but their effects are destructive. These glowing orbs send out thoughts or probabilistic fields which affect the awareness of their targets. We have lost some of our best agents during encounters with these orbs. In fact, your previous teacher disappeared due to an encounter with one.

"Sometimes our employees return to their bodies after these encounters, but their frequency is often permanently changed. We can no longer work with them. When a person's frequency passes a certain threshold, we can no longer regulate them.

"In the beginning, we tried applying our frequency regulators to the orbs directly, but that crashed the system. System shutdowns are very costly to PsyOp. We usually lose dozens of employees during each shutdown. Some affected agents return with such a high frequency that their presence alone can cause network problems. So when you see an orb, return to your body immediately, any way you can.

Now we will get your chips installed. You don't need to return to your body for the procedure, but we do need to hook you up to a frequency calibrator that will be in communication with the chip in your physical body."

Mr. Dolster tapped on his watch, and dozens of machines appeared, hovering over the students. They were covered with antennae and had intricately designed robotic arms.

The teacher continued, "These machines will install chips in the forehead of each agent. Don't resist them."

The machines started flying around the room, anchoring themselves to the foreheads of the students. One arrived in front of me and gripped each side of my head, while another two of its arms adjusted things above and between my eyebrows.

Although I was not there in my physical body, it felt like someone was manipulating my brain. Maybe I felt the chip in my body, extending its sensors into my nervous system. I wondered if they had already inserted the chip. My chest hurt, and I started to think that I probably should have jumped in front of a train while I had the chance. But then my chest began to feel cold and empty, and I stopped thinking about it. It no longer mattered to me. Nothing mattered to me. I was focused and alert, ready to do whatever was asked of me.

If my personality was a cork, someone had opened the bottle and was drinking the wine without my consent. I had agreed to this job, but I did not expect it to make me feel empty and cold.

When the machines had finished their work, they flew back to the teacher and hovered in formation. He tapped his watch again, and they disappeared.

The teacher smiled. "Nice work, gentlemen. Doesn't it feel better?"

The question meant nothing to me, because I felt nothing. The idea of feeling good or bad was meaningless to me. Even this observation of my lack of feelings was meaningless. There was nothing to compute.

Mr. Dolster continued, "Now we are ready to start working as a team. Here is how we orchestrate these missions. You will hear commands in your head, and you will see an image of your destination. All you have to do is focus on the image, and it will link you with the destination. You will instantly shift to that location. You will meet your teammates there, and you will follow the commands you receive without sharing them with your teammates. The chip in your body should be regulating the constancy of your vibration. It is relatively rare that one teammate will need to regulate the vibration of another. If everything goes well, the chip in your body will automatically call you back to your body when you encounter glowing orbs. Any questions?"

All the agents, including me, replied in unison, "No sir."

Questions were meaningless. I felt no curiosity. All I wanted to do was follow instructions. I began feeling proud that I was part of a meaningful project. Finally, I could contribute to our great country.

The teacher looked straight at me and said, "Agent 496 just had a profound realization that I would like him to share with the rest of the class."

I stood and felt even prouder. No one had noticed me or acknowledged me in a long time, and I could see now that I was finally in a place where I was appreciated. I smiled and said in a confident voice, "I am happy and proud to work on a meaningful project and protect my country."

Then we sang the national anthem together.

"That's right," the teacher said. "That's the spirit I like to see. Okay, now it is time to feed your bodies, and when you return, we'll go on a little field trip."

Everyone said, "Thank you, sir." Then we applauded.

An image appeared before my eyes. I was looking at my sleeping body from the far corner of the hospital room. I focused on my body and then woke up in my bed. I felt nothing. The only thing on my mind was that I was going to get food. I walked into the cafeteria and received a plate with my name on it. For a second, the name Greg seemed foreign to me, but then I heard a voice say, "This body is called Greg." I ate and went back to bed. Before I closed my eyes, a nurse came in. She was bringing me my daily dose of medication.

CHAPTER 6

When I closed my eyes, I saw the black screen again. I
entered and landed in the classroom. I must have come
in early. I was the only student in class, and the teacher
was wrapped in the spiral. His body shook, and there
was something that looked like a tall shadow in the
corner. It disappeared when I arrived, and Mr. Dolster's
body was released.

He looked at me coldly and said, "You came
early."

"I didn't receive a schedule. I just came back
after lunch."

"The schedule is next to your bed. It says
breakfast at 7-7:30 AM, lunch at 12-1 PM, and dinner at
7-8 PM. During those times you should be with your
body. Class starts immediately afterward."

Once everyone else had returned, Mr. Dolster
said, "I will bring you in teams to different workplaces.
Just enter the link that appears for you."

An image of a living room appeared, and I
entered. By now I was getting used to shifting through
realities. This new reality did not surprise me, nor did it
particularly interest me. I remained still and waited for
instructions. Two other agents arrived, and we waited
together. Then we were instructed to move through a
door. We glided through the door without opening it,
and on the other side was a man at a desk working on a
manuscript. Three other agents were hovering above
him, and several machines were attached to his
forehead.

Then I heard my teacher's voice. "He cannot see
you. The machines are measuring his brain waves, and
the chips planted in the bodies of the agents will be
synchronized to the brain waves. This will allow them
to align more easily with his thoughts. Before we take

action, I would like you to familiarize yourself with the manuscript."

As soon as I looked at the man's computer screen, I heard a crackling sound. It felt like I was receiving a download. Huge chunks of information entered my mind, and within a few seconds, I knew what the whole book was about. He was writing about a theory of everything based on the simulation hypothesis, or the idea that reality is information. The book quoted many recent scientific studies suggesting that mainstream science was based on an outdated assumption.

The author suggested that reality is information organized by consciousness. He considered consciousness to be an organizing energy that grows by manifesting itself in form. He connected this idea with research into children's past-life memories, near-death experiences, and out-of-body experiences. The book created a convincing argument for eternal life.

I heard my teacher's voice. "When the truth is in the wrong place it can have destructive effects. It is good for the economy when people fear death and live their life like each day is their last."

Suddenly one of the agents descended and aligned himself with the man's body. At that moment the man closed the computer and got up. He walked into the kitchen and opened the refrigerator, at which point the agent stepped out of the man's body.

The man was now cutting cheese with a long knife. Three more agents appeared and surrounded the man while holding each other's hands.

I heard the teacher say, "They are focusing on a particular outcome. Their focus affects the probability distributions of all quantum fields this man is part of. It allows them to influence the likelihood of a certain outcome."

The three agents I had seen first were above the others. They were swirling in counterclockwise circles. It looked like a dark gray tornado that was spinning slowly. They accelerated until I could no longer make out their distinct shapes. Suddenly, the three of them descended. Like water disappearing down a drain, they entered his head. The man gasped for air and then stabbed himself in the chest. Blood burst forth, splashing onto the ground. He stumbled for a few steps before collapsing.

The agents separated from his body and disappeared. I saw an image of the classroom in my mind, and a voice told me to enter. I landed back there with the two other agents that had watched with me. Most of the students were still missing.

The teacher said, "He was a well-respected scientist, and his work would have created an unpredictable ripple effect. We don't think it's a good thing to make people commit suicide, but some people aren't willing to compromise. In this case, more subtle approaches had failed us. Sometimes we need to sacrifice individuals to save the system."

He looked at us seriously and didn't say anything for a few seconds. Then he explained, "The others are watching longer missions, so I'll address them when they come back. I purposely assigned you to a very extreme example. I wanted to get a sense of where your limits lie."

As soon as he said this, I began to process what I had just watched, and a terrible feeling began to spread through my body. It was a feeling of complete doom, of utter hopelessness, regret, shame, and guilt. Suddenly I became aware of the emotions that lurked at the bottom of the cold indifference I had previously experienced. I wanted to die right there. I guess there was still a little bit left of Greg, the person that cared.

An electronic voice announced, "Agent 496 is feeling strong emotions." Mr. Dolster asked me to stand up, but he said it reluctantly, as if there were a part of him that understood the pain I felt.

Maybe "understand" was the wrong word, because the whole system was built on the understanding of fear and suffering and how to use them to obtain power and exercise control. But there is another type of understanding that is not based on rational computation. It's the type of understanding you experience when you look at your friend and say, "I feel you."

For a split second, I saw this in my teacher's eyes. It was a look of tremendous sadness. But he had journeyed too far in the other direction. At that moment he wasn't strong enough to turn around and face all the suffering he had created. Instead, he tapped his watch, and two vibration adjusters came down. The spirals wrapped themselves around both of our bodies and began to adjust our vibration. My body shook, and the intense feelings started leveling out.

While this was happening, I noticed the tall shadow again. This time it stood in the middle of the room, between the teacher and me. It extended its long arms, and its fingers merged with the energy current that was flowing around and through my nonphysical body. Before my emotions had settled completely, I felt repulsed by this figure. It seemed to feed off the energy my suffering created. It smiled and grew larger while the buzzing electricity flowed towards it. Its face was mostly amorphous, but I could still recognize that it enjoyed the process. Then my heart was cold again.

The shadow and the spirals disappeared, and I no longer cared about what had just happened. I simply waited for orders.

Mr. Dolster said, "Sit down." So I sat.

He continued, "Very good. Doesn't this feel much better?" Again, the question meant nothing to me, but I nodded because I knew that was the response expected of me.

Then he said, "You are on the path toward becoming a great agent. Now I would like you to start exercising your focus and getting used to focus aligners. I will send you a destination. Go there and follow orders."

CHAPTER 7

I saw what looked like a slum in India. I focused on the image and entered. This time there were no other agents with me, but I was indifferent. I simply awaited my orders.

All around me, people were washing laundry in a river. I heard Mr. Dolster's voice say, "Follow the focus aligner."

A translucent drone with robotic arms appeared beside me and floated toward a young woman washing a blue shirt. The machine gripped both sides of the woman's head. I heard the voice again. "Position yourself above the target."

I floated above her and waited for instructions. After some time, I finally heard, "Descend and align with the target."

I floated down and tried to align my body with hers. When my position roughly matched hers, I heard a popping sound, and I snapped into her body. She twitched a little bit but continued washing the shirt. I could hear all her thoughts. She was thinking in a different language, but I could understand the meaning. She thought about a goat her husband had just sold. She wondered if they would have enough money to buy new clothes.

I heard my teacher's voice again. "Try to get her to throw the shirt into the river. You can do this by guiding her thoughts towards something she is angry about. The focus aligner has analyzed her psychological infrastructure, and the target subject could be her sister, who did not come to her daughter's wedding. Her sister is called Raja."

I saw an image of Raja. She was a beautiful woman in her mid-twenties with long black hair and luscious lips.

He continued, "To make your target think about her sister, you must visualize Raja. Then you must increase the target's resentment simply by agreeing with it. Just say 'Yes' whenever a thought triggers resentment or anger. The focus aligner will keep running while you work, and it will give you the most updated version of her psychological responses. When her anger reaches a certain threshold, you can use that vibration to engage her physical body. Feel the anger, and then throw the shirt into the river as if that will solve all her problems. If you do this right, her body will follow."

While I listened to these instructions, I remained inside her body, passively experiencing her movements and thoughts. When the teacher stopped speaking, her thoughts became louder again. She was wondering about the clothes she should buy for her son.

I imposed my own thought: "What kind of clothes does my daughter need?" She picked up on my idea and began thinking about her daughter. She realized that her daughter did not need any clothes because she had already bought her plenty of clothes for the wedding.

I visualized Raja and thought, "Raja did not buy her any clothes." Again, she followed my train of thought, but then remembered that Raja had bought her daughter clothes a week before leaving town.

The target's thoughts went into the background, and I received an update from the focus aligner. Raja had bought her daughter cheap clothes that did not fit well. The updates from the focus aligner were both visual and auditory, like little movies. I heard Mr. Dolster say, "Try to access the resentment in her."

My target had returned to thinking about what kind of clothes she would buy for her family. She realized that her son would love a new pair of jeans. I suggested, "Good quality jeans, not like the clothes Raja bought for my daughter." She began thinking about the clothes Raja had bought for her daughter, and I began enforcing her resentment by suggesting, "Raja does not care about your family."

I received another update. It showed an image of her father telling Raja that she was his favorite daughter. My target had watched this interaction through the bathroom window when she was four years old. I focused on this moment and tried to reconnect her with the jealousy she had felt then. She picked up on the jealousy.

Mr. Dolster said, "This is a subconscious memory. She has suppressed it, but it still holds a lot of psychic energy that you can use to create the vibration you need. Keep focusing on the memory, and she will respond. Currently, this is the strongest anchor point we have discovered."

I kept focusing on the memory, and my target kept getting angrier and angrier. She was thinking in frantic circles about her sister not buying good clothes for her daughter, not showing up to the wedding, and not caring about her family.

Then my teacher instructed, "Agree with her, give her confidence, tell her that she is better than her sister. You need to boost her ego, otherwise her anger will cave in, and she will fall into passive sadness. To get her to commit to a completely irrational action, you need to increase her anger and confidence."

I began telling her that Raja deserved to be beaten, but this triggered an unexpected empathetic response. My target suddenly realized that she was dwelling on angry thoughts, and she remembered a quote from her religion: "Water the thoughts you would like to grow, grow a lotus flower within your heart."

44

This thought had an extremely powerful effect on her vibration. I heard a pop, and I was flung out of her body. A beam of white light shot forth from her forehead, and the focus aligner lost its grip. My target took a deep breath, stretched her arms, and when she breathed out, a ripple of white light blurred my vision.

I landed back in the classroom. I was alone with my teacher. He said, "Good job, 496. This subject turned out to be more difficult than we anticipated. This is the problem with spiritual practices. People can use them to raise their vibrations very rapidly, and it makes our work difficult and frustrating. If we had kept you in her presence any longer, it could have crashed our networks. We are actively working on preventing Western society from adopting spiritual practices.

"Religions are okay as long as they don't teach people how to raise their vibrations. We prefer religions that foster selfishness, hate, and jealousy.

"Our organization has been around for a very long time. Before we were PsyOp, we had all kinds of other names. We've been working with the major religions since their inception. The task is the same on all fronts. We must disguise the high vibrations of the prophets and make them look like authoritarian figures who will punish and dominate. This creates the power dynamic that is needed for the networks we're building.

"Our networks are anchored and fueled by the vibrations of fear. When a human feels fear, it's actually a certain type of subatomic organization. Particles that are part of a fear-based quantum field are all aligned with a linear type of organization. This means that the change in a few particles can be used to influence the changes in many. This is true in every type of subatomic organization, but the 'fear field' allows precise changes to be caused by the 'will' of the few.

This means that multiple choosing units are strung together by the will to protect themselves.

"Particles don't have will like we do, but they function based on probability, and there is always the question of how the probability distribution of one particle relates to the probability distribution of another. The 'fear field' does not leave this up to chance; it is precise and easily controllable.

"It's unfortunate that fear is an unpleasant feeling, because this emotion and all its emotional relatives—jealousy, hatred, guilt, et cetera—contribute to calculable and controllable fields. The higher vibrations such as love, joy, empathy, and gratitude create highly unpredictable fields. On a subatomic level, these emotions also create a very high organization, but the movement of the field cannot be controlled by one component. The love field has no set future because everything in this field contributes to the resonance of the entire field. If many people began to hold this field, the future of humanity would be completely uncertain, and our networks would be non-operational.

"To prevent humanity from entering this uncertain future, we need to make sure that the masses do not actively increase their vibration. You saw what happened when an individual suddenly confronted anger with empathy. We could no longer use selfishness as an anchor, and our networks could not compute the emotional complexity of such a response. The subatomic particles of their field all entered a superpositioned state, and from our standpoint, they were everywhere at the same time.

"How are you supposed to make any calculations if all values are infinite? It's impossible. So we're not just fighting in the name of a predictable economy, but also in the name of logic and mathematics." He chuckled a little bit.

One by one, the other agents came back from their field trips, and Mr. Dolster briefly discussed their missions with them. Some agents needed their frequencies adjusted, and I saw the shadow-being appear again to suck in their energy. I decided to ask the teacher about it.

He said, "You must be seeing things. Sometimes glitches in the data streams can create hallucinations."

My emotions were tuned down to a low gray murmur, so I accepted his answer.

I soon got used to the routine. I followed orders, manipulated people, and whenever I felt things, my vibration was adjusted. At some point, I began to enjoy having my vibration adjusted; I didn't want to feel the suffering we created.

Sometimes I had to manipulate children. Mr. Dolster sent me on a mission to give a kid nightmares and raise his overall level of fear. Apparently, he was very popular in school and was raising the vibration of his class through his positive attitude.

Mr. Dolster said, "We don't want a bunch of carefree kids to come out of that school. It's important that they adopt a functioning psychological infrastructure while they are young. Kids should be afraid of the teacher and afraid of each other. Fear isolates the individual, and that's what we need. People need to feel threatened—that's what makes them productive and predictable."

As time went on, Mr. Dolster spoke with less care. An outsider might have seen our class as some kind of satanic ritual, but we were adjusting each other's frequencies to the point that it all seemed perfectly reasonable. Seeing the dark shadow became normal too. I accepted it as a glitch in the system or something, and I no longer thought anything of it. I was just there, doing my job, protecting America, and keeping the economy going.

In the beginning, all of us wore the blue jumpsuits we had been given, even when we left our bodies. But after a few weeks, Mr. Dolster gave us new outfits. He told us, "You are now professional agents. You should dress like professional agents." So he sent us a link, and I entered.

I found myself in a clothing store with racks and racks of suits. I was alone. I surmised that each agent was sent to a different store or a separate information stream.

I heard Mr. Dolster's voice. "Touch any suit, and you will instantly be wearing it. To check out, hit *Access*."

I walked up and down the aisles, examining different outfits. Each came with a tie and black shoes, and they were all displayed in midair, as if someone were wearing them. I touched a black suit, and it snapped to my body, replacing the blue jumpsuit I wore.

Then a mirror appeared in front of me. I looked at myself, and I looked good. I still felt cold on the inside, but that coldness was now covered by a layer of pride. I guess if you are really deprived of love, a simple piece of clothing can feel very fulfilling.

I kept staring into the mirror, and I felt some form of excitement, some form of warmth, and even hope. The jacket was smooth and slick. I looked like someone to be reckoned with. My fear, guilt, and desperation were now pushed far into the background. I looked good and felt powerful.

I was part of a secret organization that controlled humanity without anyone knowing anything about it. I was dressed all in black. I could get into people's minds, pull their strings, and make them do what I wanted them to do. I was ready to fuck some shit up. I closed my eyes and focused on *Access*.

I landed back in the classroom. My teacher welcomed me and congratulated me on my new clothes. A few more agents appeared, and Mr. Dolster said, "This is a big day for you all. You are now professional agents. Let's go celebrate."

He sent us a link, and we reappeared in what looked like a huge casino. I felt more physically present than I did in the classroom. There was gravity, or at least the experience of a force that kept me on the floor. It felt nice to touch the ground with my new shoes.

Mr. Dolster pointed to the bar and said, "The bar is open. Drink as much as you like; you can't get a hangover here. Also, feel free to use the slot machines. Just enter your agent ID, and the machine will access the bank account you provided to PsyOp." I walked to the bar and got myself a drink.

I sat next to my new roommate, Adrian, but at this point, I still didn't know his name. He had short brown hair and looked a little bit Spanish. He didn't seem excited or astonished by the virtual bar. He sat still and sipped his drink.

I said, "Isn't this incredible?"

He looked at me and replied, "It's a cheap virtual reality. There are much better ones." Then he added, very quietly, "I'll show you during the next crash."

He continued talking, but now his sentences were streams of nonsense, as if to blur out what he had said before. Somehow, I knew he was doing this to hide the meaning of his words from PsyOp.

I didn't know how to deal with his intention. To me, the highest goal was following orders. I felt sorry for Adrian that he wasn't as brainwashed as I was, that

49

he wasn't proud to do as he was told, that he wasn't glad to defend his country. He wasn't even grateful for the free drinks.

I don't know how he managed to avoid detection by the frequency analyzers that seemed to be everywhere. He was good at pretending to be someone he was not. It wasn't until much later that I got to know who Adrian really was.

I finished my drink and made small talk with a few more agents. Some of them were telling me about the cars they were planning to buy when they get out of the hospital. One of them was even planning to buy a yacht. We drank a few more beers and had a few laughs. I began to find the joy in small talk. All of us had so much emotional shit tucked away that we appreciated it when the conversation stayed light.

At some point, Mr. Dolster began banging on his glass with a spoon. He announced, "It's almost time to go back, but before we start working, I would like to make a toast."

We raised our glasses, and he said, "To world domination!"

The room erupted with cheers, and we all chugged our drinks. When you have that much fear in your heart, it feels amazing to try to dominate the world. The thought was like the perfect bandage for all of us. It soothed our cold hearts and made us feel like we had a purpose. The idea of buying a nice car was now getting more appealing as well. I could drive a Mustang or something and feel like I was on top of the world.

Then we went back to work.

CHAPTER 8

I was assigned to a project in Bangladesh. My task was to influence a factory owner named Khan. I followed him around all day, floating above him and collecting as much data as possible.

His workers were suffering a lot. They were underpaid and exposed daily to toxic chemicals. Khan was thinking about turning his company into a co-op. That would mean stepping down and giving the company to the workers.

PsyOp did not like collectively owned companies. "It's not good for the market!" is what Dolster would always say. We needed to make sure that prices were kept low and that only a few people made any profit. The future that might have emerged, had Khan turned his company into a co-op, could have threatened our agenda in many ways: His friends might have been inspired by his selfless actions. Western companies buying his products would have been affected. The workers' families would have been raised out of poverty and had more free time and control over their lives. Khan's actions would have made the whole economic situation less predictable.

We needed things to stay predictable, and we needed prices to stay low. Manipulating the owner of the company was the simplest way to achieve that. So there I was, with two other agents, following Khan around and making sure the focus aligners were attached to his forehead so we could collect data properly. We needed to get a good understanding of his psychology to know where and when to engage.

To our surprise, it turned out that he was afraid of cats. Who would have thought? We used that as much as we could. We manipulated his daughter to want a cat, and we manipulated his wife to support his daughter.

The idea was to create as much friction as possible. We wanted to drain his energy and push him to give up his philanthropic goals. His wife felt neglected, so we used her fear of abandonment and tried to turn it into a desire for power. That's relatively easy work. Human psychology is designed like that. When someone is afraid, they want to feel powerful, because from an evolutionary perspective, power is associated with control and fear is associated with the absence of control. A frightened organism naturally seeks control.

We manipulated Khan into staying out late, drinking with his friends, and at the same time, we made his wife worry. We triggered her fears of abandonment. Then we made his daughter want a cat. The daughter asked her mom, and we managed to create a nice fight between Khan and his wife.

She was full of fear, worried that Khan was cheating on her, and instead of admitting her fears, she wanted to feel powerful. So she said, "It does not matter what you say, we are getting a cat."

Khan was frightened of cats but too ashamed to admit it. He said, "No way, I earn all our money. I am not wasting it on a cat."

They went back and forth until they were screaming at each other. When Khan went back to work, his hands were shaking. Adrenaline and cortisol were flooding his veins. He was still thinking about the terrible fight with his wife. Worst of all, she had ended the fight by saying, "I don't care what you say. I am buying our daughter a cat."

These thoughts were looping in his head while he was at a meeting about the co-op. He could not pay attention to anything anyone said. We kept reminding him about the cat and the conflict.

In the meantime, we went back to his wife and pushed her to buy the cat. When Khan came home, he flipped out. He saw the animal and began screaming as if a bee had stung him. He ran upstairs and locked himself in his office.

This was the time he was supposed to spend going over the notes from the meeting. He had another big day ahead of him, but he could feel none of the peace and goodwill that used to inspire him. Instead, he was loaded with hatred and fear. We exacerbated these emotions and used our tools to crystallize them into a plan.

We kept telling him to kill the cat, but he wasn't quite ready for that. We worked on the family for a few more weeks. We couldn't get Khan to kill the cat, but we created so much stress and fear that they decided to get a divorce. He had his hands full with that, and he forgot about his company and his philanthropic goals.

The operation was a success, and Dolster took us out for drinks and gambling. We had a great time, to the extent that you can have a great time while ignoring the pain in your heart and the pain you create. It became a twisted pleasure. I adjusted my frequency almost every day.

CHAPTER 9

We worked on other, more exciting projects. One of the most memorable involved a shooting and a protest.

A couple of international corporations were trying to get a trade agreement passed, and we were assigned to create drama to distract the media.

We selected Fred, a police officer in Atlanta. The idea was to make him shoot an innocent teenager. Then we would ensure that the event received a lot of media coverage and organized protests. This would distract the nation while the corporations got their trade agreements passed. We didn't want anyone to research the trade agreements and organize protests about them. We wanted to fuel the public's hatred for police brutality instead.

Hatred was another emotion that Dolster liked to incubate, especially if it was used as a distraction. It was sneaky and evil, but you get a taste for that sort of thing when you dwell in fear long enough.

There were several agents assigned to this project, and Dolster supervised us. Three agents followed Fred, and another three followed Jack, the kid who was to be assassinated. We picked him because he often walked home late at night and passed the police station on his way.

Fred was an inexperienced officer who had joined the police force to do good, but he was always scared late at night. It seemed easy enough to use this fear to force him into committing an irrational act of violence.

The idea was to have Jack borrow a hoodie from his friend, and then send him past the police station while Fred was leaving to begin his shift. Jack wasn't really an intimidating kid, but we were hoping that the hoodie would trigger stereotypes in Fred's mind.

I was working on Fred with Adrian and Agent 455. 455 was a pale, bald man with bad teeth who seemed to enjoy the work very much. He was eager to do most of the "thought surfing," as he liked to call it. Adrian and I often just sat back and watched. We still followed orders, but Dolster opted to give Agent 455 more responsibility.

Dolster dubbed him "Agent 455, the killing machine." He was proud of 455 and liked to put him to work. The whole class had turned into a perverted fraternity. All of us had gotten our heads scrambled by the frequency adjusters, and we'd lost our moral compasses while feverishly executing the PsyOp agenda.

But Adrian was different. He never needed his frequency adjusted. He was always kind of passive and followed orders, but at the same time, it was clear to me that he did not think very highly of PsyOp. Once, when Agent 455 had already returned to his body, Adrian and I were by ourselves. He said, "You know, this is total bullshit. We should not manipulate others like this."

I knew that PsyOp didn't like hearing people talk that way. It seemed to me that PsyOp had complete control over our minds, and it just wasn't worth going against them. After all, they treated us pretty well as long as we followed orders and enforced their agenda. But Adrian did not see it that way. One time, after a day of observation, he told me to wait a second.

I said, "We've been ordered to go back to our bodies. We have to follow those orders."

Adrian said, "We don't have to follow shit! Are you really buying into this PsyOp mind control bullshit? Try to remember who you are!"

I didn't know what to say. The concept was too large for me to consider fully. So much of my personality was beyond my control at this point that it was impossible for me to have controversial thoughts. Plus, Adrian still hadn't even introduced himself properly—I knew him only as Agent 039—so I was surprised to learn that he knew my real name.

He said, "Greg, stay with me for a second."

Hearing my real name startled me, and it gave him enough time to say a few words.

"Look," he said, "we're safe for a couple of minutes. Their networks are really not that stable. If you work for them long enough, you'll figure out how to take advantage of all the glitches and flaws. We have a few minutes before they'll be able to detect our late arrival. Greg, I want you to work for the other side. There are many beings from other galaxies that are willing to teach us about the truth. The shit we're doing for PsyOp is no good; it only pushes you further into delusion and fear."

I didn't really listen to what he said. When he said the word "PsyOp" it felt like an iron claw had pierced my back and gripped my heart. I was terrified. I said, "I have to go back to my body now."

I focused on the link that was still flashing in my mind, and I landed in my body. Adrian landed in his body a few seconds later. We didn't say anything more to each other. We walked to the cafeteria and ate in silence.

At this point, I was going through life like a sheep. I felt like I'd had more of a personality when I was homeless; at least there had been things I believed in and I'd felt genuine emotions. Now my personality was splintered into a million pieces, and I did things because I was told to do them. It seemed impossible to put all my experiences into one bucket and say what was actually going on. Without thinking about it, I had decided that I was doing a good thing for my country, and that meant following orders no matter what. But working with Adrian was making me uncomfortable. Something in his eyes challenged me to question my beliefs.

Later that night, Adrian and I were observing Fred again. We were running focus aligners on him, trying to find more psychological triggers. The holographic machines were attached to his head, and they were probing his brain with their robotic arms.

Adrian and I sat back watching Agent 455 rub his hands together with anticipation. He was excited to dive into Fred's body and play with his mind. Adrian shook his head and did the bare minimum that was asked of him. He must have figured out how to maintain some of his individuality while staying under the radar. I didn't have the freedom to hold my own opinion. Morals and feelings had lost their meaning.

After several days of observation and planning, Agent 455 entered Fred's body and walked him out of the police station. Agent 455 was perfectly aligned, so Fred noticed nothing except that he was scared.

An agent from the other team went into Jack's body and began walking him home. Jack wore his friend's hoodie and walked towards Fred. This triggered Fred's fears. Agent 455 made him grab his pistol and shoot Jack three times in the chest and once more in the head.

When the body hit the ground, Dolster appeared and clapped his transparent hands. He said, "Congratulations, Agent 455! The killing machine!"

Agent 455 separated from the officer's body and showed his bad teeth in an ugly grin.

Just then, I heard a sarcastic laugh and saw the shadow again. It floated above the crime scene, and this time I saw its face clearly: It was a hideous version of myself.

Before it disappeared, a thought flashed through my mind about how overwhelmed I was with doubt about this path I had taken. For a split second, I realized I was becoming something else. I was becoming someone my mother would not have wanted to sit with at the dinner table. But the thought left my mind as quickly as it had entered, and I returned to my cold and indifferent state.

We left the scene and let the confused officer deal with the situation. There were some bystanders, and one of them had called an ambulance, but the boy was already dead.

Next, we focused on a few news outlets, some left-wing activists, and a judge. After a heavily manipulated trial, the police officer was found not guilty, and the activists freaked out. We guided them towards anger, hate, and violence. We got a few of them to light cars on fire.

The protests we helped orchestrate were spectacular, and we got some great news coverage. Meanwhile, the corporations passed their trade agreements without anyone noticing anything. The whole nation was focused on the injustice done to Jack. We were playing people like pawns while digging our souls' graves. But fortunately, I did not get sucked any deeper into this dark hole.

CHAPTER 10

One day, I remembered Joey. I was in a conference room with Dolster, talking about the next project he wanted me to work on. I sort of drifted off into my own thoughts. I remembered one of the last things Joey had said to me: "I wanted to show you what is beyond."

As soon as I remembered those words, Dolster looked at me and said, "What was that? We detected inconsistencies in your data flow."

"Oh, I just remembered what my friend told me. Go on."

Dolster said, "We are adjusting your vibrations in relation to this experience. We need to straighten up the inconsistencies these associations create in your field."

This seemed perfectly reasonable and logical. The focus aligner appeared and placed its robotic arms on both sides of my head. Then Dolster asked, "What does Joey mean to you? The name holds a lot of psychic energy in your field."

"He was my friend," I explained. "We used to live together on the streets. We shared the money we made each day and drank beers together. He was going through some trouble, and one day he jumped in front of a train. It almost killed him. He spent months in the hospital, and that was where he learned how to meditate. When he came out of the hospital, he was very nice to me and taught me all about meditation. He brought me food and encouraged me."

Suddenly, I felt intense gratitude, and Dolster said, "Stop. Your vibrations are no longer workable. We need to adjust you."

The spiral came from the ceiling and began wrapping itself around my body. Dolster said, "We will help you forget about Joey."

With a flash of light, a glowing orb appeared. It floated between Dolster and me, radiating an intense energy that appeared to be melting the spiral. I watched each ligament disappear. Like fireflies dissolving into a golden mist, the robotic structure of the spiral merged with a strong current of white light and then vanished.

A reality-dissolving wind seemed to emerge from the glowing orb. The walls and chairs of the conference room lost their shapes, and the only things left were me, Dolster, and the glowing orb. White fog surrounded us.

The orb emitted a thought: "You can choose in what truth you stand." It was so powerful that it rattled the core of my being. The orb continued, "We are now standing in the middle of our truths. You still have your physical appearances, but I do not. I can also meet you at your truth."

As the fog settled around us, the orb transformed into Joey. His long blond hair covered his shoulders, and his blue eyes met mine without fear or confusion. Joey said, "Now I will show you my truth."

The fog rose again, and when it settled once more, Dolster's form had dissolved into a million screaming heads.

Seeing this, I felt like I was falling off a cliff. Images flashed before my eyes. I saw all the people I had manipulated, but worst of all, I felt their emotions. I felt their confusion, their fear, their desperation, and their anger. I felt guilt and remorse beyond words.

I wanted to die, but I knew that that would not be enough. I had to change. I knew at that moment that I couldn't hide from fear any longer. I could not go on like this, perpetuating fear and misery in the name of a healthy economy.

The wall that PsyOp had placed in my heart was now broken. I was screaming and crying as the pain entered my heart. I wasn't in my body, so there were probably no tears running down my cheeks, but the energy of complete desperation and regret shook my soul.

I saw only blackness, but demonic forces seemed to swirl all around me. I could feel their long slimy fingers reaching for me, but a stronger force permitted me to glide past them. Gradually, my surroundings brightened, and thoughts of forgiveness entered my mind.

These thoughts did not say, "It's okay to harm people." They said, "The light gets to know itself through the darkness it believes to be." They were filled with the purest form of understanding, and they were the energy that was making me glide upwards.

I realized that guilt and shame weren't going to mitigate the suffering I had caused. I understood that I couldn't know myself without totally forgetting who I am. I suddenly saw all that had happened as necessary. Now there were new, strange beings around me. They were amorphous mixtures of plant and animal, and they radiated a very encouraging energy.

As one, they said, "Yes, you have forgotten who you are, but we will keep you awake and guide you." I listened and felt their warmth, and gradually, the moment became all that was. I was pure light, aware and full of love.

Slowly I became aware of the conference room. It seemed like time had frozen. I was in the same situation as before. Joey, disembodied as a glowing orb, was in the middle of the room, and Dolster was still a dark amorphous blob of tortured faces. But my perspective had changed. I was buzzing with love and gratitude.

Although Dolster looked very scary, I didn't react with fear. I understood that his appearance was a metaphor for the pursuit of fear. Thoughts and realizations were flowing freely between Joey and me, but Joey pronounced them and let them ripple through the conference room.

Joey said to Dolster, "Your field is constructed from the suffering of others. In the truth of love, everything is connected, and the tip of the pyramid becomes part of the energy on which it sits. This is why you now experience the suffering that you created. This is not punishment; it is simply the truth from which you have been trying to shield yourself. You are part of a larger field that is made of the entangled particles that all your actions have ever created. In Hinduism, they call it *karma*, but you will understand it better in terms of entangled particles and the probabilistic or vibrational fields they create. Experiencing this truth gives you a choice: face it or invest more energy in the constructions of delusions. The choice is yours."

Dolster was still a morphing mass of tortured creatures from which screams and foul smells emanated. I couldn't hear or smell it as much as I could feel it. The essence of suffering leaked out of his almost formless appearance.

Joey spoke again. "What you are going through right now is good, as long as you consider the word good to mean that which brings harmony to all of existence. You have used the word good to refer to things that aligned with your agenda. But your agenda was not based on the essence of your being. Who are you beneath the mask with which you have identified? You might consider yourself a powerful being, capable of living in multiple realities at once, capable of manipulating others. But all the networks or realities that you have created are experienced by you, and who is that 'you' that experiences your reality? Have you ever asked yourself this question?"

Dolster had now turned into a ball of black smoke. Occasionally it would condense, and a tortured face would reappear, speaking a few words that sounded more like the hissing of a snake that someone had stepped on.

Joey shifted back into human form and reached into the black smoke, pulling out a tiny glowing ball. He held it in his hand, pressed it against his heart, breathed into it, and then morphed back into the glowing orb. The two orbs merged into one, and for a while, I saw only white light. Then the fog settled again, and the outline of the conference room reappeared.

Dolster was back in human form, as were Joey and I. Dolster looked very different. His face and his body were the same, but I could no longer imagine him teaching class or supervising missions. He looked startled and out of place. After a long silence, he said, "I haven't been home for a very long time. I forgot that I have a home. I forgot who I was. If I only knew that the networks were keeping me . . ."

"It's okay," Joey interrupted. "At times, we all forget that our home is eternity and that we are eternal beings. We have all pursued a destructive path at some point."

Suddenly, several glowing orbs appeared and surrounded the three of us. They were connected by thin streaks of light, and I could feel and hear a warm humming. The tone was a form of communication. There were no words exchanged, but we all resonated in a field of understanding transmitted by the orbs. The understanding was a welcoming into the world of love, a welcoming into eternity. We were congratulated for piercing the delusions of fear and aligning ourselves with the vibration of love.

I noticed that Dolster was glowing. Several streaks of light were attached to his body. I realized that they were adjusting his vibration, but instead of lowering it and aligning him with fear, they were allowing him to vibrate in gratitude. He joined their hum, and Joey and I did too.

For a long time, a humming and glowing mass of light filled the room. This was the last thing I remembered before I woke up in my hospital bed. I could see the flashing image behind my eyelids again: "The networks are down."

CHAPTER 11

I sat up and saw that Adrian was also sitting up in his bed. He looked directly at me with a huge smile and said, "They're down again! Want me to show you my favorite virtual realities?"

I was a little unsure how to respond to his enthusiasm. I said hesitantly, "Sure."

"What's your agent ID? What number did they give you?"

"They call me Agent 496."

"Cool, I'll send you a destination."

An image appeared. It said, "Agent 039 would like to send a link." Underneath were two buttons labeled *Allow* and *Decline*. I looked at my roommate and asked, "How did you do that?"

"I'll explain everything later. We don't have much time, at least not here."

For some reason I trusted him. I focused on *Allow* and said "access" in my mind. I heard the popping sound, and I was standing in an empty white room.

My roommate appeared beside me and said, "Hi, I'm Adrian. Sorry I didn't introduce myself earlier. I just wanted to get out of Earth time as quickly as possible so that we could use this opportunity. So how much do you know about the networks?"

"Nothing, really. I'm fairly new."

"Okay, I'll explain it to you. Right now we're talking at a normal speed, and we could talk for 10 hours before one second passes in the hospital room. But this is not because of Einstein's relativity theory. It's actually much simpler.

"Think of it this way. Our physical universe is all information that updates itself every Delta T. Delta T is the smallest measurable unit of time, but it's created or driven by a larger reality that runs countless other universe simulations. We don't know much about this larger reality. Some people think the glowing orbs come from there, but we can't prove it because they use too many variables with an infinite value. Some people speculate that there is no such thing as time at all.

"Anyway, it's still a big mystery. But what we do know is that there are countless realities running at different time scales. You can't travel between them with a physical body, but if you leave your body, you can log into these realities like joining an online computer game.

"PsyOp only lets us use the networks for work, but when their access system is down, we can log in without being detected. Let me show you around. I know a bunch of realities you would enjoy. Where do you want to go first, sex or adventure?"

"Um . . . I don't know, man. I'm just . . ."

"It's only a tour," he interrupted. He sent me a destination, and we entered.

We found ourselves standing in front of a swimming pool. Next to us were two undefined shapes that looked like human-sized green holograms. Adrian said, "Here we can choose who we go out with. I'll send you a link, and you can select the pictures you like."

I saw images of beautiful women, and whenever I focused on one, two buttons appeared that showed *Submit your choice* or *Get more selections.* After browsing for some time, I found a girl who looked just like the prostitute I used to see in New York. I submitted my choice, and the undefined shape took on the characteristics I had selected.

She greeted me with a friendly voice. Her name was Anna. Adrian was already sitting at the pool, but he was alone. We joined him, and the three of us ordered drinks from a waiter.

I asked Adrian why he didn't pick a woman. He said, "The water, the palm trees, the air; they are my girlfriends."

I looked at him, confused, and changed the subject. "Is everything here a simulation? Are the waiter and Anna just the products of a computer program?"

He said, "Don't think about what is real and what is not. You're here to enjoy yourself, and perhaps to learn a few things. Everything you do here only exists as an experience, but if you want to get deep about it, everything you do is just an experience. I selected the pool and the waiter before we came here because I thought you'd like to experience them."

He waved over the waiter and ordered a round of shots.

I asked Anna, "What's this simulation stuff all about? Do you care at all that you're just a simulation?"

She said, "Do you care about the fact that you're a simulation?"

"But I still have a body in another reality."

"You're saying that you have an entry point to a simulation that you consider more real because the laws of time and space maintain a consistent relationship between actions and reactions. That's just a different data system, but you're no more real than I am. It's a matter of perspective."

"Hmm . . . okay, I guess." I felt somewhat dizzy, and no one was telling me what I should or should not do. That gave me a mild sense of anxiety. It felt strange to be able to follow my curiosity. Then I thought of a good question for Anna.

"So what happens to you when we leave?"

"I no longer exist as an individual. My consciousness will go back into the system that created me."

"You die?"

"No, I cease to exist as an individual."

"How does that feel?"

"It feels great."

"I can't really imagine what you're talking about."

"Well, individuality is a temporary state of being. I also identify with the data flow of the whole system that is giving you this experience of being at the pool. I'm all that is now manifested as a specific being that's in service of your awakening, of the process that will allow you to also know yourself as all that is. But since you're at a certain level of identification, I'm here to meet you at a pool."

What she was telling me reminded me of Joey. When he taught me how to meditate, he also talked about a lot of spiritual stuff, which had seemed irrelevant at the time. Now I wished that I had paid more attention. I was feeling a little uncomfortable because nothing made sense and I was free to do what I wanted.

I turned to Adrian and said, "Where are we? Is this reality created by PsyOp? Who runs this system?"

Adrian said, "Nah, I got this destination from one of those glowing orbs during a recent shutdown. I asked them if they could give me access to a reality where I could enjoy beauty. The orb told me that they only use form-based realities to learn. But they gave me this one and said I could enjoy and learn at the same time.

"I was just confused because PsyOp was not really into this kind of thing."

"You mean into being yourself without worries?"

"I guess so . . ."

Anna moved closer to me and whispered into my ear, "Did you know there are layers and layers of beauty beyond your ability to appreciate?"

I asked Anna, "What are those layers?" She took my hand and placed it on her upper leg. Her legs were smooth, and I felt a tingling in my pelvis.

Then she said, "Is this the only way you can enjoy this?"

"Um . . . what do you mean?"

"Can you only feel this in your lower energy centers?"

"I don't know what you're talking about!"

"Sex. I am talking about sex. Is sexual desire the only way you respond to female beauty?"

She began to rub my leg and said, "We can have sex, that's not the issue. But I would like to show you the many layers of beauty that are beyond the desires and fears female beauty triggers within your mind. Do you want to explore this in privacy?"

"Ah . . . um . . . I guess?" I was unsure about everything. I wished she would simply tell me what to do.

"Okay." She said to Adrian, "Just send him a notification when you want to leave."

She took my hand, looked into my eyes, and I could see an image of a bedroom. She asked, "Did you get my invite?"

"Yeah."

"Okay, see you there."

I entered and landed in a bed next to Anna. She was naked, and candlelight illuminated her body. She looked beautiful and relaxed, but I was nervous.

She told me to lie next to her and close my eyes. I followed her instructions. A million thoughts entered my mind so quickly that I could barely identify their meanings.

Anna said, "So normally you would probably jump on top of me, cum in a few minutes, and talk about meaningless things until we both fell asleep. But this is only one layer. To get to the deeper layers of enjoying the beauty of love, you must clear your channels. Right now, they are clogged by the social norms of your society.

"Many subconscious fears are attached to the topic of sex. If you grew up on Earth, you will certainly have picked them up. Perhaps from the way your family reacted to the topic, or from your teachers, friends, and partners.

"Whenever you encounter the topic of sex, you also encounter a tightness in people's bodies. This is why your heart is beating so fast right now. This moment is triggering all your fearful subconscious memories. Maybe you think you need to do a good job. Or maybe you're afraid of a woman who speaks her mind. It doesn't matter what the reason is. Just be right here with whatever you're feeling and know that it is perfectly fine. You are like a growing plant, and where you are right now is the tip of your leaves. This is where you're at, and you can only start from where you are."

She placed her hand on my chest and told me to breathe into my heart. My heart was still beating really fast, and I was battling thoughts telling me that I was not manly enough, that I should be the one helping her. Then I began to blame myself. Here I was in bed with a gorgeous woman, but I was preoccupied with my anxiety.

Anna said, "Let me help you. None of these thoughts serve you, and you cannot hide them here. You cannot be anything other than what you are, and by trying to be something that you're not, you only make it more difficult to be what you are. If you let yourself be who you are, you will discover that you're never one thing. Everyone and everything is dynamic, constantly changing, and anxiety results when you try to resist your dynamic nature and try to be what you think you should be. Right now, you are nervous. Why not be authentic and just be nervous? This is how your body would like to express itself right now."

"But this is not even my real body."

"There is no real or not real. Everything is real from the perspective of the divine. Nothing is real from the perspective of the small self. You are here, right now, interacting with information based on the habits you have accumulated. That is real. You are in a bed, and you are separate from it—that is not real. Don't overthink it. You're here now, experiencing what you are experiencing.

"Right now, you're next to a naked woman, and this makes you nervous because your field is used to a certain sequence of events. In the past, events like this were traumatic, and this trauma is still lodged in your field. You must release this trauma to access the deeper layers of sexual pleasure. But saying that you *must* let them go might be counterproductive, because it creates a goal and then a value system with which you can judge yourself even more harshly. Let's give up all goals. There are no goals. You do not have to please me, and you don't have overcome your own fears. We are just here, and that's it."

As soon as she said this, I felt energy flowing out of her hand and into my heart, spreading through the rest of my body. In an instant, I was less concerned

71

with myself. I felt that she accepted me exactly as I was.

I began to truly appreciate Anna. She was wise, kind, patient, and beautiful in every way. She kissed my cheeks softly. Her warm, wet lips were sending shivers down my spine, and I could feel a different kind of energy beginning to circulate through my body. I was confident and aroused.

I placed my hand on her stomach and then slowly moved it down until my fingers found a spot that seemed to please her. She sat up and placed both of her legs alongside my body. She moved her hips up and down very slowly, letting me feel every part of her. She put her hand on my chest again and said, "Try to keep feeling your heart as well. Keep your energy circulating through your entire body."

I felt sensations I had never felt before. My whole body was tingling with joy, and every breath seemed to go through every part of my body. For a long time, Anna and I stayed connected in this intimate way.

Then I received a link from Adrian. I said goodbye to Anna, and she told me that I could come back whenever I liked to see her again. I asked her how to save the link, and she said, "That's right, you're new to this. Adrian can help you. Just ask him. He's a good kid." I thanked her and kissed her goodbye. I entered Adrian's link and landed in a desert.

He said, "Welcome to the desert! Ready for another adventure?"

"Sure, but before we start, I want to ask you something. Anna told me I could visit her again, and that you can show me how to do it."

"Someone fell in love?" He laughed and said, "Sure, I'll show you, but that can wait till we get back to the hospital. Right now, I want to show you some crazy shit. This is another link I received from an orb.

Some of the stuff here is really beyond my understanding, but it is definitely entertaining. Apparently, this data system evolved on Earth but was separated from our reality before Europeans took over America, Africa, and Australia. The timescale of this reality is roughly one year per second, so one year passes here while one second passes in our reality. We could raise a family before we have to go back to our bodies."

Adrian laughed again. "But life here is really beyond what I can understand. I will try to explain what I know. There is this nonphysical network that connects all life, and it merges with the physical reality in a really weird way. Well, technically, everything is nonphysical, but I call it physical because it appears physical. I mean, our reality is also nonphysical, but it appears physical. Anyway, this reality we're in now has this other layer that ours has too, but PsyOp doesn't exist here. Instead, the networks here are governed by all living things. PsyOp has mapped out what it knows with reason and logic, but here it's all very ambiguous and mysterious.

"All tribes that ever lived here became this giant nonphysical tree which you can visit and explore. But they're labyrinths of experiential realities themselves. Last time I was here I got stuck with this tiger for what felt like ages until I finally lost all my fear of it. If you're scared to death for, like, a month, your fear kind of dies.

"What happened was I walked into this plant, and it led me into a cave, which then closed behind me, and I was stuck inside with a tiger. It was terrifying because I forgot that I had a body in another reality. I hope nothing like that happens to us this time, but I also don't regret it.

"After being in there with the tiger for a very long time, it eventually turned into a human being. It said he was my grandfather from another life and he wanted to help me deal with my fear. He said that he was living in this version of reality because he wasn't interested in the experiment I was a part of. I asked him what experiment I was a part of, and he said, 'Forgetting who you are and getting scared to death.' I told him that I wasn't interested in that kind of experiment either, so he asked me, 'Why, then, were you afraid of the tiger?' As I said, this reality is totally crazy. I thought I would give you a heads up before we get ourselves into some serious shit here." He laughed again.

I said, "I don't know, man . . . that sounds kind of unpredictable."

"Yeah, that's the whole point of the adventure. Come on! We have nothing to lose. Time here really doesn't matter. Even if it takes us sixty years to find our way back, it'll cost our bodies only a minute."

"Dude, I am not about to get lost for sixty years. That is totally crazy."

"Why not? It's one minute. Think of it this way: you can live a lifetime in one minute. Doesn't that sound fun?"

"No, dude. Sorry, I am not going to do that."

"Okay, you wait here. In sixty years I'll come back and give you the link to get out . . . if I still remember it." He laughed and said, "I'm just joking. If you really don't want to do this, we can leave. But before we go, let's talk to a plant, so that you get a feel for the place."

"Okay."

CHAPTER 12

My body seemed very real. I could feel the sand under my bare feet and the sun on my shoulders. I was wearing an unusual outfit made from one long piece of white cloth that wrapped around my body. Adrian was dressed identically. I looked at him and asked, "What's the deal with these clothes?"

"That's just how people dress here. Just trying to fit in, you know?"

"Where are the people?"

"Not here."

"Obviously."

Adrian laughed. "Well, like I said, shit is weird here. I don't think anyone lives in this part; it's just the entrance to their world."

We walked towards two large dunes and began climbing over them. From the top, we could see a small lake surrounded by palm trees and plants. Adrian pointed and said, "All those trees and plants are doorways to the ancestor tree. It's the tree where all the spirits of this world live. These spirits have been around for millions of years and have evolved together with the plants. As I understand it, each plant holds a field within which the consciousness of a tribe resides. It's confusing, but you'll see what I mean when we get there."

The dune was very steep on the other side, and we slid with each step. When we reached the lake, we knelt and drank from it. Plants and trees surrounded us. Adrian said, "Let me see if I can find the plant I want to show you."

We followed a path, and eventually, he bent down in front of a small fern. He touched the plant's leaves and said, "Please allow us to access your worlds."

The plant began to move. Its leaves spread out, and it looked like another leaf was growing from its center, but instead, a transparent ball emerged. The ball separated from the plant and swelled until it was nearly as big as me.

Adrian looked at me and said, "Crazy, right? Now we have to jump into this ball. This place doesn't use links; everything has a more natural and mysterious feel. It's a different design. Ready to jump?"

"No way! What if I forget who I was?"

"Oh no, this just brings us to the beginning. I'll warn you if we get to those parts."

"We just jump into the ball?"

"Yeah. You can run into it or just jump in."

Adrian ran towards the ball, and I followed him. The sounds around me died down, and it felt like I was falling into a dark bottomless pit. After plummeting for what felt like a long time, I began hearing drums, shakers, and voices.

We were still falling, but I could see again. We appeared to be falling parallel to a massive tree trunk. The bark was brown, but a white glow emanated from cracks in its surface. For some reason, we were now slowing down, and I could see the tree more clearly. Within the lit places in the bark, I could make out a thick forest. The tree seemed to be made up of many smaller trees, or many experiential realities within which trees and plants covered mountain ranges. They looked like entrances into different universes within the patterns of the glowing bark.

Adrian told me that each branch was inhabited by countless generations of tribal spirits. He said that their consciousnesses manifested the jungles and the light that emanated from the bark of the tree. We were moving very slowly by now. Adrian pointed to a branch and said, "This is where Umbumi lives. Want to meet him?"

"Who is Umbumi?"

"He knows this place well. Let's go see him."

"I don't know. Is it safe?"

"Dude, what are you so worried about? Your body is in a fucking mental hospital, and you're working for some stupid organization that can't even build the simplest networks correctly. I mean, look at this shit! This is a functioning network that has evolved for millions of years. Why do you care so much about the reality where your body is parked?"

"Because . . . what if my body dies?"

"Your body would survive several days without your spirit, so theoretically we have thousands of years in this reality. But don't worry about it. We're not going to stay that long."

"Okay, let's check it out, but warn me before I get myself into something unpredictable."

"Of course."

We floated closer to the tree. It was so tall that I couldn't see the bottom or the top. Even the nearest branches extended farther than I could see. White fog enveloped the jungle plants. It looked like we were coming to the shore from the middle of a big river. We floated towards what looked like a crack in the ancestor tree's bark. We climbed up vines until we were in a thick jungle. I turned around, but the entrance was suddenly gone, and the jungle extended in both directions.

I panicked and begged Adrian to open it back up. He said, "Relax, man. This is how things work here. They're weird. I told you."

"Yeah, but you also told me that you would warn me before we got trapped here."

77

"Dude, I'm just going with the flow. I had no idea that the entrance would close up like that. Look, things work differently here. You have to go with the flow, and then things always work out. If you resist or panic, that's when you'll get stuck. Act like a plant. Keep your cool and match the vibe of the place. Otherwise, your fear will get the best of you."

I tried to distract myself. I could still hear the drumming, but now it was louder. The sounds were more crisp and distinct. The more I paid attention to the sounds, the quieter my thoughts became. I noticed that all the plants around me were moving ever so slightly, like the sounds were winds moving the leaves.

I too began to move. Dance seemed to be the natural state of this world, and I let it affect me. I turned to Adrian, whose body was also moving to the beat, and I said with a smile, "Oh man, this place *is* crazy."

"Yeah, it's amazing when you align with the vibration here. It's like a party drug. Let's follow the sounds."

We were still drifting through the jungle, but without conscious effort. Everything happened on its own. I felt weightless. We passed through some thick shrubs, but the leaves and branches also moved to the sound and bent smoothly around our bodies, as if they were already expecting us.

We entered a clearing and saw several beings dancing around a purple fire. The creatures were roughly human-like, but very different. Their faces changed with the beat. It almost looked like they were wearing masks, and they also looked like they were part of the fog. They shifted in and out of physical form.

When we got closer, I realized that the fire was coming out of their feet, and the pulses of the flames appeared to be created by their dance. Suddenly, they stopped dancing and turned to us. The fire went out.

They stared with piercing eyes. One of them stepped forward and touched his chest while he said something in a foreign language. I didn't understand the words, but I knew what he was saying, as if there was an underlying language of intention that we communicated telepathically.

He welcomed us to the land of the ancestors and introduced himself as Umbumi. He said, "I see you are from a different womb; you are from our mother's sister."

Adrian said, "Yes, our information system has branched off yours and is evolving at a slower rate."

Without opening his mouth, Umbumi said, "We can leave words behind. The language of intention is preferred here. The beat of the ancestor tree synchronizes our minds. We can always understand each other."

I still heard drums in the background. The source of the sound was unclear. It seemed to come from all directions. My mind was very calm, and Umbumi's thoughts seemed to be part of the music. The plants, the drumming, the air, and thoughts all seemed to be part of a vibrating energy. Then a question formed in my mind, and it felt like it was part of the music too. "Why did our information system branch off from yours?"

Umbumi said, "You have seen the tree we are part of. This tree is part of a larger tree, and your universe is a part of a different branch—the patterns continue. But of course, there is not really a tree or a branch."

Adrian looked at me and said, "The tree and the branch are visual representations of information systems that have older versions in common."

I asked, "But why do they branch off?"

Umbumi answered, "To explore different paths."

I was overcome by curiosity, and I continued to ask questions. "Why though? Who or what is deciding what paths are interesting, and how fast they should evolve?"

Umbumi said, "Akalele decides." As he said this, the image of a glowing orb appeared in my mind. He said, "This is the purest form of Akalele that you can understand. But Akalele is everywhere, it is that which makes you breathe, and it is that which makes the drums beat, the drum in your chest and the drums of the earth."

He stomped his feet and the beat intensified and I began to see purple light radiating from his feet. He reached down and picked up a handful of purple light. It dripped from his hands like a liquid. He continued, "Put this on your chest. This is also Akalele. You might understand this way."

I took the purple light from him. It tickled my hands, but it was weightless. When I placed it on my chest, I began to gasp for air and quickly inhaled. The purple light was sucked into my chest.

In an instant, I saw my life flash in front of my eyes. I saw myself as a kid at preschool. I saw all my developmental stages unfolding like reverse origami. Significant interactions were brought to my attention, but I could see them from a different perspective.

An inherent understanding accompanied all my memories, and I saw how the search for love took different paths. I understood that even the cruelest people were attempting to get love and share love, but what made them seem evil or mean were their impossible strategies.

Then I saw all of it from an even further removed perspective. I saw how the people of my civilization were attempting to work together, but they were using an impossible strategy. Everyone was trying to get things by taking them, not by giving them.

I saw my civilization evolve. Inventions created in response to suffering contained new potential. That potential looked like a tree that was growing towards the sun, but the leaves were made of glowing orbs. I understood that the orbs were unique and contained the emotional patterns they had collected during their lives as human beings.

Then I heard Umbumi's voice again. "Everyone sings their own song, and together we sing our mother's song." I understood that every problem and every tragedy was part of the evolution of unique patterns within consciousness, or Akalele, as Umbumi called it.

I was still experiencing the insights from the purple light I had inhaled. I understood that every experience was like a clay pot, a container for Akalele. Then I saw that I was in a clay pot; I was part of a soup Umbumi and his tribe were cooking. I was observing all this from the third perspective. I saw the giant pot being stirred, and then the soup suddenly became white light. Soon, there was nothing but light, and I felt nothing but love.

I heard Umbumi again. "Your life is the container for the light you are making. You are light, but you are also your light, the way you stirred the pot, the amount of pepper you added, what kind of wood you used for the fire. All those things are the experiences only you had. Your soup is your song, and when you recognize your soup as light, it can be eaten, and then you can sing your song while others sing their song. Our mother's sister is trying to sing her song through you. You are part of her song, your song is her song, but you cannot sing it yet, and she cannot sing it yet. You are in a hospital bed, and her vocal cords are clogged by machines. Her soup has gone bad, and we want to help her stir the soup, add more fresh ingredients so that we can sing together. You are a fresh vegetable we would like to add, but before we can add you, your pot needs to be stirred and your song needs to be sung. Do you understand? If you want to be part of this, say 'yes.'"

I agreed without hesitation. What Umbumi said was intellectually confusing, but a deeper part of me knew what he was talking about; the feelings were familiar.

The fog settled, and I was in the jungle again. Adrian was next to me, and Umbumi still stood in front of his tribe.

Adrian said, "They see our data system as family, and they want to help our networks become what they can be."

I asked Umbumi why our networks had evolved the way they had. Umbumi said, "Disease is a corrupt pattern."

All at once, I found myself in another data stream. I saw an infinite number of figure eights. The two loops of each figure eight connected to the loops of four other figure eights: one above, one below, and one to either side. Gradually, the figure eights morphed into snakes that had their tails in their mouths.

I heard Umbumi speak. "You see the order, but now watch and see what happens when one snake breaks the pattern and bites the snake beside it."

The pattern began to unravel as the snakes defended themselves against one another, and soon it became a writhing pile of fighting snakes. Eventually, the stronger snakes started organizing the weaker snakes into piles. They picked them up by their heads and carried them to the piles. To my surprise, the weaker snakes within the piles revolted and began attacking the stronger snakes.

I realized that Umbumi was showing me the history of my civilization. The image transformed, and the piles of weaker snakes became slaves and the stronger snakes became imperialists. I was once again next to Adrian and Umbumi.

Umbumi said, "Our tribe branched off before that snake bit the other snake. Akalele wanted to explore a path where that action did not happen. In our reality, Europeans never gave up the tribal life; they never got infected by the insatiable desire to control and conquer. We are still vibrating in harmony with all plants. The reason we are evolving faster than you is so that we can share our wisdom with you. Our soup has already been served, and you can eat it too. If you know what good soup tastes like, you can add the right ingredients to your own soup."

I felt energized and eager to learn. I asked, "Why and how did PsyOp get to control our networks?"

Umbumi said, "The networks are not separate from the pattern. They are part of the pattern. The fight for dominance also continued there. Slaves used their ancestors for black magic. It was their only tool against the imperialists. This created an organization based on hatred and fear, which the imperialists eventually learned to use for their own advantage. They call it PsyOp now.

"The imperialists never understood that they are an expression of Akalele. Instead, they thought that they were the pot and not the soup. They thought they were the mouth and not the song. So our mother's sister has lost herself and still believes that she is an unhappy white man that needs to dominate the world. But she is beginning to find her way back to her ancestors.

83

"There are many trees that are sprouting, and even some that have already begun to fruit. Your friend Joey has already fruited. He is singing his song. Our sister's mother is beginning to sing her song. Soon she will sing more, and you will be heard. Your song will be part of her song. But before you go back, we would like you to live one life here. What do you say?"

I began to understand what he was saying, and the idea of living a life here was no longer terrifying.

Adrian looked at me with a big smile and said, "We could be brothers!"

I happily agreed. The idea of living in this world was suddenly very exciting.

Umbumi said, "Before you can bring the right information back with you, you have to live it, you have to experience it, you have to find yourself in the light of a healthy tree. The Akalele within you forms habitual patterns. When you live a certain way, that pattern stays in your Akalele. Then you can bring that pattern with you. You will not know about it, but you will be it. The Akalele in you will speak to the Akalele of those around you and transmit the information on its own.

"You have come to us because the Akalele within you wants to express itself in a way that we have cultivated. You want to experience our dance, and your soup will be cooked in our pot. Your song will be the merging of many patterns, and one of those patterns is the dance that we have cultivated. We will watch you from here and guide you through the most valuable path that we can see. It might be challenging because you have many, many patterns that don't belong here. Fear and greed have eroded the harmony of your Akalele."

I saw the image of fighting snakes again.

Umbumi continued. "Those are within you, and when you are back in a body, they will seek to express themselves. But they cannot go very far here. We offer them no resonance. We do not sing their song. They must learn to sing our song, and that will hurt them greatly."

Adrian and I looked at each other. We were nervous but also excited. I felt a shiver of determination.

"Okay," I said. "I think we're ready." Adrian nodded in agreement.

Umbumi said, "Do you want to choose a life, or do you want us to choose for you? From where you are right now, you cannot fully understand what is important. I would recommend that you let us choose for you. You will both die as wise old women."

"Women?" Adrian asked.

"Yes, women. You cannot understand this now because the overemphasized masculine patterns of your culture are clouding your judgment. Through the body of a woman, you will receive the most relevant lessons."

I became doubtful and thought about whether I should just go back.

Umbumi had somehow produced a mirror, and he held it up to me. I looked into the glass and saw a woman with dark skin and green eyes. Her gaze seemed to call, "Come, be me . . . become me."

I felt an irresistible urge in my chest. I looked at Umbumi and said, "All right. Let's do it."

Umbumi touched his chest and lowered his head. Then he turned to his tribe, who still stood behind him in a circle. They began stomping their feet and singing in unison. The purple fire once again burned between them, and when the flames were high, Umbumi turned to us and said, "Jump into the fire! Jump!"

Adrian ran towards the fire. I followed him. The flames hit me with a dull pain that made me want to

85

hide under a blanket and be angry at my mother. But that idea began to hurt me too, and every other thought that followed caused an aching as well.

I wanted to hit someone, but the pain became unbearable, and I felt like I was falling down an elevator shaft. I could hear my screams getting lost in infinite depths, and I could no longer see a thing. Then something that felt like a net caught me, and I tossed and turned in excruciating pain.

Suddenly, I could see again. I had landed in a pile of snakes. I tried to scream, but I couldn't make a sound. Something was stuffed into my mouth—it was my own tail! I was choking on it, but I couldn't remove it. All the fighting and struggling simply hurt too much, so at last I surrendered.

I saw that I was linked to other snakes, but the image faded slowly until I was perfectly still and no longer felt or thought anything. I had no memory of having ever been anything else. I was just there, in a peaceful ocean of absolute nothingness.

Forms began to emerge. Below me, I could see a few straw huts in the center of a clearing. I floated towards one of them, passed through the roof, and found myself hovering over a pregnant woman.

The woman looked at me and said, "Welcome, I am happy to have you as my daughter." She didn't open her mouth, but I could feel her intention. She was filled with generosity and love. She placed both of her hands next to her belly and said, "Come in, my daughter."

Then I was in a dark place, but warmth and love filled me with comfort and joy. A few months later, I was born into a small community. I had no previous knowledge of anything else, and even the strangest customs seemed normal to me.

We didn't eat food or drink water. We got our nutrition by vibrating with plants. We didn't wear any clothes, either. For warmth, we vibrated with plants. The solution to every problem was always vibrational. If someone got sick or felt weak, we helped them by dancing and singing.

My best friend was a girl from the next village. Her name was Arilla. We spent a lot of time vibrating together, singing, dancing, and exploring the depths of plant wisdom. There were no goals, but there was a lot of curiosity, gratitude, joy, and all kinds of love.

One evening, I was sitting by a purple fire when one of my mentors spoke to me without words. Later, I learned that her name was Armassa, but at this time, I perceived her as an ever-present vibration. She was a nameless thought, but at the same time, I knew exactly how to communicate with her. She was within the trees, within the stones, and within the fire.

I talked to her by looking into the fire. My gaze was fixed on the wavering flames. She told me that my Akalele wasn't just mine. She explained that my Akalele belonged to all that had ever been. When she said this, an arm extended out of the fire and gestured, forming a circle in the air. She said, "You are all when you know who you are, but even when you did not know who you were, you have been many things."

The arm disappeared, and the fire began smoking heavily. The smoke formed spiral patterns, and within the spirals I began to see the face of a turtle. I felt a pulling sensation, and I found myself swimming along the pebbles of a riverbed.

Initially, my consciousness was dreamlike, in the sense that I didn't question the experience. I was gliding past aquatic plants, moving my legs minimally. My hard shell gave me a feeling of safety. Then I came across a bright-purple aquatic plant. As I swam closer to the plant, it felt like I had woken from a dream, but I remained within the turtle's body. Then I remembered my conversation with Armassa, and I could feel her presence as she continued her explanation.

"You have been a turtle many times, long before you wanted to experience the challenges of human life. Your Akalele is a collective project, and your current state of awareness is a product of the experience of many plants and animals. When you spend time being a plant or an animal, your Akalele gets shaped by the dominant tendencies of that being. For example, being a turtle has given you the tendency to be passive, to accept things as they come your way. A turtle does not have many predators and lives a long and peaceful life. You spent several lifetimes floating in streams and grazing on the bottoms of lakes. But your Akalele also chose to explore the life of a honey badger.

"This has created an interesting imbalance; you are passive and peaceful, but also violent and courageous. The lives of the turtle gave you the tendency to go with the flow and accept life as it is, whereas the lives of the honey badger gave you the tendency to challenge what is. In a human body, you can use the complexity of the intellect to bring those tendencies together and mold them into something more fluid. The culture of the ancestor tree has helped you do this very gracefully, but in other lives, where you grow up in a less harmonious environment, the opposing tendencies within you can cause a lot of trouble. Finding solutions in unusual situations is what keeps the growth process of your Akalele interesting."

As she said this, my turtle body began dissolving, and I found myself staring into the flames of the purple fire again. My long black hair hung over my breasts. A patient, benevolent silence filled the air. My attention slowly shifted to the sounds around me. I heard insects chirping in the trees.

Then my mentor stepped out of the fire. She showed me one of her bodies—it was purple—and she spoke. "Listen to the insects, for you too have been an insect."

Armassa picked up a handful of dirt. She slowly opened her fist, and as the dirt slowly fell to the ground, she said, "Life is in everything. Akalele is in everything. The dirt is also having an experience—not as complex as that of an animal or a plant, but everything is structured by awareness. The awareness of matter isn't as individualized as that of animals, but the patterns that form within matter have the potential for the perception of an individualized self. This does not mean that you are better than dirt, only that you can learn from the dirt. You can go back to where you came from. You can become all things and still be an individual, because one individual is part of all things. Akalele is on an infinite path of exploring its potential to shape information through the different modes of identification."

I spent many nights with the fire, with the trees, with the sounds around me, and with whatever wisdom wanted to reveal itself. Arilla was there too. I found her occasionally in the forest at night. She liked digging holes, kissing the dirt that hadn't seen the sunlight in years. She taught me how to plant seeds and honor their growth process. But I preferred to spend time with the fire. I had learned to ignite flames without burning any wood. The creative element of my imagination was the spark that ignited the flames. Sometimes I would sing and dance all night while listening to music the fire wanted to share with me.

Eventually, I learned the balance between individuality and shared awareness, like a pendulum gracefully touching extremes. I learned to think and feel like the soil in the ground, while seeing the forest from the perspective of a bird. In the end, I retreated into my stillness as I became the wise grandma who helped the young and healed the sick. I watched my grandchildren grow and play in the dirt. I taught them how to sing and how to dance. I taught them how to align with the vibrations of plants and speak to the ancestors who were waiting on the other side. When my skin was wrinkled and thin, my hair white, I heard the voice of death calling me to step through the vail. Arilla and I both knew that we were linked beyond this life, and that this village was only a small step on a long journey. Together we said goodbye. One after the other, we jumped into the purple flames and woke up on the other side.

Umbumi greeted us with open arms. I had seen him in my dreams and had many visions of him, but only now did I remember that I still had a body waiting for me in a hospital. All the conversations came back to me, and I thanked him with all my heart. I felt a certain stillness through which I could now see his beauty more clearly. I could feel his wisdom in my own chest.

He said, "I see your Akalele is now aligned with our mother, and it is now time to bring the medicine to her sister."

I felt the truth of his words, as did Adrian. We looked at each other with sparkling eyes and felt the gifts in our hearts. We were ready to bring them back.

Umbumi said, "Don't forget, you are diving back into a corrupted network, but you will know what to do. Your vibration will guide you. Step out of the way and let your Akalele unfold. In time, everything will be in perfect clarity."

The jungle opened up, and white fog came pouring in. Umbumi said, "Go into the fog. A ball will bring you back."

We said goodbye and disappeared into the fog. Something lifted us, and we came out beside the small fern that Adrian had contacted a lifetime ago. Our footsteps were still there.

I asked Adrian, "How long were we gone for?"

"We definitely lived several decades in their time zone, but our footsteps are still here. Maybe no one walks around here, or there's no erosion, or maybe the faster time zone starts within the ancestor tree. Whatever the reason, we were probably gone for under ten minutes."

"Well, let's go back now. Maybe you can show me how I can visit Anna on my own."

"Sounds good."

He sent me a link, and we both woke up in our hospital beds.

I got up and went to the bathroom. I felt like I was a new person. Everything around me radiated and glowed. I could sense the vibration of peace flowing through my chest and through the furniture in the room. The desk next to my bed appeared to have a friendly personality, and the floor seemed infinitely patient. I took slow steps and listened to the sound of my feet as they touched the ground.

When I came back from the bathroom, I looked over to Adrian's bed. He was stretching his neck. He said, "The networks are still down. Want me to show you how to visit Anna?"

"Yeah, that would be great."

"Each information system and all of its networks are always accessible to all users. You actually don't need the programs PsyOp gave us. They only provide them to control their employees. Accessing networks is easy when you aren't afraid. It's only the fearful beings that need to gain access artificially. PsyOp has assumed that fear will always

91

exist; they haven't figured out yet that it's just a stage in the evolution of consciousness. That's why their networks are crashing so much. Akalele, or the larger mind, has begun growing beyond fear, so PsyOp is fighting an uphill battle. All you have to do is stop fighting this battle and surrender with trust. If you let everything go, if you let yourself die, then you're reborn in your natural state. Trust that you can access anything you want."

I closed my eyes. What Adrian had said was a bit vague, but I knew what he meant. I focused on relaxing and trusting that I could access any reality.

I still saw the blinking image and the words "The networks are down." But I recognized that it was only a thin layer of myself that agreed with this perception. Underneath, I began to see millions and millions of snakes, all curled up in a highly organized pattern. I relaxed into this pattern in a way that is hard to describe. The metaphors dissolved, and I found myself in empty space with no visual perceptions. Then I simply made a wish: "I would like to see Anna."

I heard the popping sound, and I was at the swimming pool. Anna was sunbathing in a blue bikini, her body glistening with oil. Her lips were moist, and she smiled gently. Her body radiated like a diamond, bundling together the essence of plants, flowers, and mermaids. The energy she emanated reminded me a lot of the vibrations we worked with at the ancestor tree. Now I could see her more clearly.

I lifted my hands and reflected her beauty back to her. I felt a sensation of love in my pelvis and my heart. I added my energy to the beauty Anna radiated, and she began to moan. I took deep breaths and added the vibration of the air to the current that was flowing between us.

I felt the ancestors' drumming in my heart. It spread through my whole body, and I saw purple flames emerging from my hands.

Anna's body twitched as her moaning intensified. I held her in my arms as she experienced multiple quaking orgasms. Tears flowed down her cheeks, and we both stared into each other's eyes. Without words, we acknowledged the limitless beauty of existence. Here we were, both in form, yet drawing from a source beyond it. This source was our willingness to be completely present with each other, without fear or expectation. The palm trees around us were in agreement. I could feel them dancing to our song.

Anna whispered, "Thank you for facing your uncertainty and allowing yourself to be open to the beauty that has always been."

The vibration of this thought rippled through the swimming pool, and Anna kissed me on my lips. Her hand wandered down my chest and found a comfortable spot between my legs. Waves of appreciation spread through my body. She undressed me and moved her underwear to the side. Delicate lust unfolded as her glistening flower took me in.

Without moving much, we created a current that traveled up my spine, out of my heart, into her heart, down her spine, and out of her pelvis. I held her tight and kissed her neck.

We rested in deep orgasmic love and watched the flowers giggle. My heart blew her kisses until I felt that it was time to go back.

I no longer needed links. My intention to return to my body was the means of transportation. One reality seamlessly morphed into the other, and I opened my eyes in the hospital.

The networks were still down, but the blinking sign no longer bothered me. I could align with it and see it, but I could also shift my attention without being distracted.

I didn't know what to expect next. Would the networks come back online? Would there be a new teacher? Would they try to adjust my vibration?

CHAPTER 13

That night the networks came back online. I aligned myself and entered the classroom. It was only about half full.

Adrian was sitting next to me, and to my surprise, Dolster was there too. He was radiating a completely different energy. Something about his face had changed, and I thought his eyes held some of Umbumi's kindness.

Dolster said, "My dear students, I'm on a different path now, and all of you who have shown up today are coming with me. Whether you know it or not, you have chosen to come to this class in service of a higher frequency. There are many layers of the self, and we're not always conscious of all of them. The part of you that has decided to come here wants to realign with the truth.

"For the last two months, we have pursued the delusions of fear. We have manipulated others to enforce the agenda of the military-industrial complex. We will no longer be doing this. Instead, we will help society to be reborn at a higher frequency. Instead of manipulating, we will guide, encourage, and awaken. But before we can help others, we must help ourselves. We have a lot to learn, which is why we are in the classroom today. You all need to be re-educated.

"We may need to confront some aspects of PsyOp, but it will be difficult for them to reach this classroom. We now exist on a vibration that would instantly crash their networks. Many multidimensional beings have helped us rebuild the networks in a higher octave. The work is not complete, but since we're building within the vibration of love, the new networks are already much more secure and resilient. They cannot crash, because they're not centralized.

"Each one of you is a provider. Each one of your consciousnesses is creating the vibration within which we experience this classroom. We all contribute to the field of love within which we work now. We do not require a centralized organization; we have entered a frequency that unifies diversity through the consciousness modality of love.

"We grow like plants. We grow like the forest. We are like a fungi mycelium. We contribute to the network by helping each other. This form of organization is much stronger than anything created by fear, but this is not to say that we won't face challenges. If all of us were to become afraid, we would lower the vibration of this classroom. If we are possessed by fear, PsyOp can reach us again and use our consciousnesses for their purpose.

"There are still very powerful forces that depend on fear, and they may try to make us agree with their delusions. This classroom is a small boat on a huge and dark ocean, but the dark ocean is a tiny puddle in the infinite ocean of love. So do you understand where we are now?"

Adrian and I both resonated in agreement, but the other students were somewhat confused.

"Don't worry," Dolster assured them. "All I'm saying is that we have to think really, really big—bigger than the massive walls that pretend to be the end of everything there is. They are not. They are tiny cockroaches that should be stepped on. Sorry, cockroaches, I'm not trying to insult you. The point is that these manipulative walls of fear only appear big and terrifying. They are not.

"They want to force you into a situation in which you agree with them. They want you to say, 'Yes, you speak the truth. Please protect me.' But fuck that. Excuse my language, but honestly, fuck off. Let's say it together: Fear, go fuck yourself! Everyone now with me. Fear, go fuck yourself! Fear, go fuck yourself! Fear, go fuck yourself!"

We repeated this phrase together for nearly a minute. At first, it was awkward, and some of the students laughed. What was even more surprising was that no voice spoke up to warn that our emotions were becoming too heightened.

"Now let's take a softer approach which is equally powerful," Dolster suggested. "Let's say, 'Fear, it is okay. I love you.' All together now. Fear, it is okay. I love you. Fear, it is okay. I love you."

Again, all the students participated.

"Now be still," Dolster continued. He looked around the room and asked, "What do you think now? How did that feel?" He pointed at a young man sitting in front of Adrian and said, "I can read your vibration. You were thinking, 'This teacher has lost his mind.' Correct?"

The young man said, "No."

"No? Interesting. It must be my own fear that is creating thoughts of paranoia. It's a fine line and an important question: when do you trust your intuition? Ideally always, but fear can also creep into your mind and give you the most devilish paranoia, especially when you're working towards disempowering your fear. Let me show you."

He looked frantically around the room and said in a tense voice, "So, so, so . . ." His jaw moved like he was trying to spit out a cockroach. Suddenly, he stomped and screamed, "Come out!"

I saw the shadow again. It still had my face and was looking at me with an evil grin. It whispered with a voice that appeared to originate within my own head. "I am your dark self, you still haven't faced me." Then the image became distorted and disappeared.

Meanwhile, Dolster was coughing up black smoke. The smoke poured from his mouth and began taking on a physical form. It looked like a rabid ferret that had been run over by a truck and left to rot for several weeks. This disgusting creature was gnashing its razor-sharp teeth as it emerged.

Dolster held it in his hand and said, "Here you go. This is my fear. If I'm frightened of it, I feed it, and then it becomes bigger and more terrifying." Suddenly he looked scared, and the creature began to grow and wrap its human-like hands around his neck.

As Dolster gagged and gasped for air, he whispered, "Now I will give it some love, and you'll see what happens."

He whispered, "I love you, fear. It is okay. I know you're scared, I know this is the only way you know, but you can trust me. I will take care of you. Don't worry, I love you, fear. I love you, I love you. You too will grow towards the light, and I will help you."

The creature's terrifying features became less distinct as it shrank and reverted to a small, barely significant cloud of black smoke. Dolster reached into the smoke and pulled out a tiny white ball of radiating light. He held it in his hand and whispered to it, "You are the seed that I will keep watering. Don't be afraid, I will take care of you. I will keep watering you, and I will keep loving you no matter what. I will make you grow and allow you to become a big glowing orb."

He inhaled the ball of light and what remained of the black smoke. He said, "I have a lot of fear in me, but it's no longer in charge. I have lived for a very long time oppressed by the kingdom of fear, and I have led many beings into the depths of darkness. All my actions linger in my energy field. The black smoke is a visual representation of the organization that fear creates. I have a lot to work through. I need to restructure all the patterns that I have created. I have many wounds to heal, and this is the path I now follow. I ask the fear to show itself, and then I love it unconditionally.

"Love is like water, and fear is like soil. When you water the soil, a plant can grow. But fear is afraid of love because it thinks that it cannot trust it. It's afraid to be disappointed, to be blamed, to be accused, to be punished. It needs love desperately but is afraid to ask. Instead, fear pretends to be strong and scary and tries to take what it needs. But what it needs cannot be taken— it must be given. So it's really at war with itself, even though it doesn't want to admit that. It would rather take the whole universe down into the darkness of its endless craving and suffering."

Dolster looked thoughtful for a moment, and then he said, "Enough about fear. Let's talk about love. I would like to introduce you to a guest speaker."

There was a flash of light, and a glowing orb appeared. It was a beautiful ball of white light radiating comforting warmth. It had no face, but it was as if I could see a friendly smile in my mind.

A thought rippled through the classroom and entered everyone's mind.

"If you look at our universe from a physical perspective, you will find planets, stars, galaxies, and so on. But each planet is not just matter. It is also alive, in the sense that it contains the potential to build complex systems that we recognize as organisms. What drives this evolution is consciousness, which is essentially a nonphysical energy that extends through all that exists. If you want to be technical, everything is nonphysical, really, since matter is just organized information. But for the sake of simplicity, let's call it the physical universe, and consciousness we will call a nonphysical energy.

"So we have two intertwined layers of reality: the physical and the nonphysical. You can also look at them as patterns with different degrees of density. They influence each other through the process of reincarnation and evolution. Consciousness takes physical form, identifies with organisms, and tries to express its creative potential by expanding the complexity of physical organisms. In the process, organisms evolve and so does consciousness. But just like any dynamic system, the feedback loop between consciousness and physical organisms can get out of hand. Consciousness can become fear-driven and evolution can become dominated by the idea of 'survival of the fittest.'

"You see, evolution does not need to be conflict-based. It can also be fueled by love and cooperation. This is what the essence of consciousness truly desires. Expressing love, or the will to benefit others, is not just a romantic ideal, it is the essence of our potential. Collaboration and symbiotic relationships can form very high-level organizations—the highest, in fact. But this is less likely to emerge in a given system. This is why consciousness creates many universes, or many experiential realities, and explores many different possibilities.

"Consciousness comes from a formless reality and incarnates into these limited information systems we know as physical realities. In the process, it organizes itself. It becomes love consciousness, which is a type of consciousness that is capable of building highly harmonious information systems with other conscious agents. When every being in a system wants to benefit every other being, the system achieves a high level of organization.

"We dip into form, and after we learn enough about interactive relationships, we go back into our formless realities and create things you cannot imagine. We are all formless, but not all of us have recognized ourselves as formless consciousness. Many of us still identify with the psychological patterns of our physical existence.

"What really binds us to the limitations of physical existence are fear and desire. We are afraid of losing something, we are afraid of danger; or we desire fame, recognition, pleasure, wealth, and so on. But all those things do not really exist. They are illusions that we learned to believe in during our physical lives. Our essence is eternal and cannot be destroyed or harmed. Physical pleasures can never truly fulfill us, because what each of us really desires is the expression of our truest self, which is eternal, which is love, which is our creative potential.

"Fear is a belief that has evolved in response to death, but death is also an illusion—it is not real. Fear evolved because organisms that were afraid ran away from danger and protected their physical forms. It was necessary for physical survival, but from the perspective of our eternal self, fear makes no sense. It is based on the denial of our eternal existence. So here we are in the middle of the battle between our eternal nature and our identification with a finite existence. This struggle is a pattern that repeats itself wherever this relationship between form and consciousness exists. But you don't need to see it this way to be aligned with it. You don't have to put it into these specific words. We are talking here about a way of being. You don't need to be able to explain it. When you know who you are, you know who you are, and you will naturally want to serve others.

"If you look at the history of humanity, you can see how this higher consciousness has visited Earth many times. It has inspired multiple cultures and religions, but it has never managed to create internationally collaborative systems. For the first time in history, we are now entering a time in which it will be possible to permanently anchor this vibration."

As he was saying this, the holographic blackboard lit up, displaying a three-dimensional image of Earth without any clouds. Waves of light illuminated the planet. The orb explained that the flickering light illustrated fluctuations in consciousness.

It said, "Here you can see how the quality of consciousness changed over the last five thousand years. Small pockets of humans have reached very high levels of consciousness at different times. But the cultures these beings created were destroyed by wars. The higher-evolved beings then chose to incarnate on other planets, or other versions of this Earth."

A different slideshow began. We saw an Earth-like planet surrounded by a purple glow.

The orb said, "This is a planet in a much older galaxy. The beings here have already managed to form an internationally collaborative civilization. Many beings that outgrow the human experience go here next. They also forget what they were before, but all the virtuous tendencies they have accumulated during their human lives are also compatible with alien civilizations. Everything is information, even the essence of a being is information, and that information can move to different planets and different information systems. The essence of a being is relational; the way you put your cells in a relationship with one another determines what kind of human being you become. What your soul learns during this process can be transferred to many different life forms."

The orb paused for a moment and then asked, "Do you have any questions?"

Adrian raised his hand and asked, "What's the difference between a planet and an information system?"

"Very good question. Well, planets *are* information systems, but some realities that consciousness inhabits are not planets. Higher-evolved beings live in very open-ended realities. The more love there is, the more freedom there is. Beings can live together without time and space as long as they all try to benefit each other. In some realities, thought creates matter. You think about something and it becomes real. You can only enjoy this kind of reality when your mind is very pure. That is why it is so important to work on yourself and gain control over your thoughts and emotions. This is what it means to raise your frequency."

The orb spoke to us for a little while longer, but eventually, Dolster said it was time to feed our bodies.

I reconnected with my body and walked to the cafeteria. I didn't feel as good as I had a few days earlier. My joints felt stiff and my head was cloudy.

I remembered the things the orb had said, but I couldn't really feel them. It was hard to feel love in this hospital. I had so much old emotional pain latched onto my flesh and bones. There had been moments when everything was bright and beautiful, but now I lacked any gratitude for my body. It felt like a burden to be identified with this human organism. It was hungry, and it demanded that I walk it to the cafeteria.

I got in line, picked up a plate of food with my name on it, and began to eat. It tasted like frozen food that had been microwaved, and a slimy sauce coated the vegetables.

Who makes this food? I wondered. *Why does it have my name on it? Does each person get a different meal?*

I looked at Adrian. He was sitting beside me, eating the same thing as me, but the person next to him did not have any sauce on his plate. I looked around the room and realized that Adrian and I were the only people with sauce on their vegetables. I found that strange. Maybe PsyOp had realized that our class was now on a different course. Maybe they were trying to prevent us from joining the new networks.

Then I saw the shadow float across the room. It still carried a perverted version of myself as its face, and it laughed and grinned in the creepiest way imaginable. The shadow disappeared again, and I was left with my thoughts.

I wondered if the sauce contained chemicals to make me more fearful. I had no idea how PsyOp was run, or how they reacted to the incident with Joey, which had caused an entire class to leave the curriculum. PsyOp did not seem like the kind of organization that would simply say, "Whoops! A whole class of agents is now being educated about raising their frequency. Oh, well." Almost certainly, they were already planning a counterattack. There was no way they would give up unless the recent crash had shattered the whole system.

I looked at Adrian and whispered, "We're the only ones who have this sauce on our food."

He said, "I know. Don't eat it."

I left it alone, but before I could get up, a guard approached and said, "Eat your vegetables."

I said, "I'm not hungry."

Adrian mumbled something I didn't catch.

In a tone that sent shivers down my spine, the guard said, "Remember why you are here." But we still didn't eat the sauce, and he turned his back and walked away.

Back in our room, Adrian fell asleep without saying anything. He probably headed straight back to class, but I wanted a moment in this reality to think things through.

CHAPTER 14

The experience at the cafeteria had left an uneasy feeling in my chest. I didn't think I was being needlessly paranoid. PsyOp had shifting gears and was now trying to control us by putting chemicals into our food. What if they took our bodies while we were in class? They could do anything they wanted with us. Neither of us had families; no one would investigate if we disappeared forever. This had to be why they targeted homeless people with dead parents.

The whole thing gave me a bad feeling. It didn't feel safe to leave my body. Maybe that was the point. This feeling was PsyOp's attempt to prevent me from raising my vibration. Maybe the whole interaction at the cafeteria had been staged, to push me back into fear and paranoia. Maybe I wasn't frightened enough to work for them any longer, or to get connected to the frequency adjuster.

The thing about living in multiple realities is that it gets confusing. You don't know who's invested in what, and you don't know the scope of the playing field. I had no idea how deep PsyOp's reach extended. My interactions had been with the branch that anchored itself in human reality, disguised as a defense strategy, but all the shit I was experiencing was making me think that something much more sinister was at play. What was this shadow that I kept seeing? Why did it have my face? It seemed like there were deeper routes that PsyOp never mentioned.

It was all fucking with my mind. Who was I really, and what the fuck had I gotten myself into? I felt taken advantage of. This organization took homeless people and totally scrambled their minds. If I knew it was going be like this, I would have chosen to stay in jail.

This thought brought some kind of finality and emptiness to my mind. I felt hopeless and powerless, and after a while, I settled into a very comfortable state of surrender.

I heard a soft whisper. "Come to class." It wasn't really a voice, more like a suggestive thought.

I closed my eyes and accessed the classroom. I landed in a chair and saw a crazy creature giving a lecture. It seemed to be shifting in and out of physical reality.

Dolster sat in the far-left corner with his legs crossed, his eyes fixed on the creature where it stood in front of the holographic blackboard.

The being said, "I have claimed my formless existence as a Blue Avian, but I have been human before. I know your struggle well. It is a common one."

The paranoia and fear I experienced earlier was now a distant dream. The Blue Avian's movements and words filled the room with warmth and comfort. It was hard not to smile.

The Blue Avian went on. "I have come to this class to expand your understanding of the nonphysical reality. But before I continue, I want to show my gratitude for this opportunity." It gestured to Dolster and said, "As some of you know, Dolster has made a very courageous choice to open his class to the interdimensional community of light beings. We have come to your planet to help you grow out of fear and transcend form. You are supported by many intergalactic and interdimensional civilizations. It is an honor to come as a representative of the Blue Avians. Like many of the more advanced races, we have joined forces with unity vibration. We identify as love, and we exist mostly as nonphysical beings, but we can also use form when it serves a purpose.

"This is the last physical body I used, but as you can see, it is only a shimmering resonance pattern of light. I am showing myself like this because I choose to. I am not confined to one body or any other manifestation of myself. So here I am in my light body that was once more physical.

"I wasn't always the shimmering being I now know how to be. A long time ago I believed in the physical nature of my body. I thought that body was real and represented all that I was. When I was born into that body I could not alter it with my mind. It was like a prison. But slowly I learned to align myself with unity vibration, or the truth of love, and through alignment with love consciousness, I have learned to transcend form. Now I work mostly with the nonphysical layers of our civilization, and I visit younger civilizations to help them grow beyond fear and delusion. Now let's get started."

The Blue Avian lifted its wings and smiled. It began to shimmer brightly, and waves of light washed through the classroom. It felt so good I wanted to scream with joy. The creature lowered its wings again and said, "This was the understanding that pierced through millions of years of suffering. Like all other beings, I have suffered an incredible amount. I could spend hours telling you about human lifetimes in which my children died. I was tortured, burned at the stake, beheaded in front of my children, enslaved, raped, and more. I suffered a lot as a human being, but I also suffered as an alien, or as a different form-based being. There is conflict on many planets, and I wasn't always the victim. I also tortured other beings, oppressed them, dominated them, manipulated them, raped them, and killed them. I have been deep in the delusions of fear.

"Suffering is surprisingly similar across civilizations. That is because consciousness builds similar free-will systems. When multiple free-will units interact within a rule set, such as time and space, they must always decide how to treat the wills of other beings. Younger civilizations go through tremendous suffering before they align themselves with love. Love is a harmonious consciousness modality based on benefiting others. But a civilization can only evolve to this place when all beings work on their own consciousnesses.

"Younger civilizations can never solve their problems by manipulating or dominating the will of other beings. The solution needs to come from the eternal self within each being. This is because each being is in fact divine and holds within itself the potential of a harmonious civilization. By divine, I mean that it has a mysterious essence that cannot be understood with three-dimensional logic.

"Consciousness is a creation of another dimension. It is an energy that is not defined by beginnings or ends; those things are perceived by consciousness, but they don't give rise to it. Consciousness comes from beyond, and we can align with its potential through thoughtless love. But don't mistake love for the beliefs our minds have fabricated. Love is a thoughtless energy, beyond belief, beyond identification, and beyond separation.

"When the members of a civilization align themselves with this energy, political problems and social problems solve themselves. Humanity's problems arise because humans choose to align themselves with the identifications of form, which are fear, selfishness, greed, and violence. You can only be afraid, selfish, greedy, and violent if you believe that you are a physical being with a finite life. As soon as you claim your eternal identity, those lower vibrations fall away, and the problems you used to have will no longer exist.

This is why we are here now, bringing you the teaching that will help humans go beyond the identifications of form.

"We will teach you concepts that can be understood within time and space, but we will also give them to you as vibrational transmissions beyond form.

"These teachings have been expressed in many different ways, but the essence is the same on all planets, civilizations, and levels of perception. This is because these teachings bring beings back to their origins, and all beings come from love. Beyond all universes, beyond all form, beyond all creations exists a field of love. This love is timeless, but it is in love with the creations of time. It enriches itself through universes and the beings that evolve within them. There are countless evolving realities and countless beings trying to find their source while wandering blindly through the mazes of time. Their blind wandering brings them to discoveries, to new ways of being, and eventually they share their gifts by realigning with their eternal selves.

"All of us have an insatiable craving, which we express in different ways, but what each of us wants is to find our self. Our true self is not human, is not Blue Avian, is not any specific race. Our true self is divine. It is love. We find it by applying the teachings to ourselves. Let me show you."

The creature lifted its wings again and moved them slightly, like an eagle about to take flight. A massive shockwave rippled through the classroom. Everything lost its physical appearance, and for a moment, all of us were steeped in the buzzing energy of complete unity. It was hard to put into words because it was not a linear type of experience. We were just there, with no thoughts, no worries, immersed in what I could only call the recognition of eternity, the recognition of our eternal selves.

Slowly things settled, but before the being took on its birdlike shape, I saw that it had transformed into a brightly glowing orb. Unlike the other orbs I had seen, this one was glowing a bluish-white color. It gradually morphed back into the shape of a Blue Avian, and I could see the classroom again.

The being lowered its wings and said, "In this reality, this classroom, we are again in the illusion of separation. The illusion of form. You are in front of me, and you are different from me. You have your own thoughts, I have my own thoughts, and that's how we communicate and perceive one another's individuality. We know now that beyond this way of being is an infinite ocean of light. This knowledge is really the heart of the teaching. It puts everything into a different perspective. All your worries and fears are suddenly less real, less important.

"The games we play here in the illusion of separation are the rivers that flow into the ocean. The experiences we have in separation add to the ocean of light. Every thought we have, every emotion we have, every action we take, they all shape the intricate waterways that flow into this ocean. The water picks up minerals along the way and enriches the ocean. It is not pointless to be trapped in a body and believe the things your psychological infrastructure is telling you. All those experiences are valuable and important. Let us appreciate the experiences we have here, even if they are difficult and painful.

"Would you recognize love if you did not experience the absence of love? It is this balance *between* unity and separation that teaches us how to find unity *in* separation. Eventually, it becomes a dance. You can dissolve into the current of love that flows through everything that is, but you can also pull yourself back together into a more contained unit. Both states have their advantages.

"When my individual identity is totally dissolved, everyone feels me, and I feel everyone. My creative energy is equally distributed among all beings, and I might ignite a spark in a few receptive people. But when I am back as an individuated unit of consciousness, I can choose where I put my energy. They are both beautiful states, as long as they are not separated by fear. You see, if you fear that you cannot let yourself dissolve into everything, you will contract and resist the process. On the other hand, if you get too attached to unity, you become afraid of separation, and that creates resistance. The key is not to resist any state of being. It is all an oscillation, a wave of different experiences. I can tell you this, but for you to internalize this knowledge you must go through whatever you have to go through. There is no quick way around the obstacles of fear. However, it is comforting to know that these obstacles are only there to help you grow. They are the game you play with yourself. A good rollercoaster needs to seem real for you to enjoy the ride.

"You grow by experiencing your fears and desires. Most beings do this by engaging in situations that they find desirable or frightening, and by experiencing these situations, they realize that what they want is beyond transient ways of perception. We all crave eternity, and when we discover eternity within ourselves, we have found our true home. You wake up and say, 'Wow, that was a crazy ride.' Once you are awake, you will no longer feel the need to play the game of desire and fear. This is why the Buddha, one of your human sages, was content sitting under a tree. He discovered the teachings by observing his own mind.

He woke up from the dream of desire and fear and said, 'I am awake.' If you say, 'I am here,' it is the same thing—you claim your eternal nature. Those words resonate with your essence and align your self with the teachings.

"Let's do it together. 'I am here. I am here. I am here.' Through these words, you are surrendering to the divine as you. When you say these words, you permit your eternal self to be here as you. Your time-and-space-based identity becomes a piece of clothing that you offer to your divine self, to your eternal self, to your true self, the part of you that is aware. If you agree with the claim 'I am here,' you will not be ruled by fear and delusion anymore. But this does not mean that you will face no further challenges. When you claim your eternal identity, you will begin to lift your time-and-space-based self, or your small self, to a higher frequency. This is often a tumultuous process, because many parts of your small self still operate within the frequency of fear. To outgrow them you need to remind yourself who you are: 'You are here. You are here. You are here.'"

CHAPTER 15

The Blue Avian went on preaching like that until it was time for a break. Then the hard part started again. I woke up in an angry body. There was a whole chunk of my personality that could not agree with a preaching alien. Why me? And why now? How was I supposed to deal with this shit without losing my mind? I was still Greg, the tough guy who wasn't willing to admit that he had no control and didn't know what was going on.

It felt good to be upset about the situation. It felt familiar. I got to experience Greg, the guy who wanted to drink a six-pack and get in a fight. But now I was in a mental hospital, going to class with aliens, while feeling justifiably paranoid about a secret organization that had planted a chip into my body. There were no beers to drink and no mental curtains to draw. I had to come to terms with my situation.

PsyOp had gotten into my mind and taken everything out that could have caused resistance, but now there were other forces at play. The dam had broken, and the water was gushing in. I had to face the truth, and that made me angry. I sat up and clenched my fists. I wanted to punch something, but instead, I began to breathe heavily. The oxygen felt good in my body, and some clarity returned.

I realized I was angry at myself. Why had I gone along with all this nonsense? The word *nonsense* echoed through my head, and in its wake, I found a moment of silence. I realized that it was too late to turn around and dismiss everything I had been experiencing. It was too late to accept that I had gone crazy. I had experienced something that was more powerful than anything my mind could tell me.

There wasn't much left of my normal reality. I was barely even using my body; it was more like an angry flesh machine I had left behind. There was no way I was going to take that as my only identity and my only reality.

This thought calmed me. It put things into perspective. Knowing that it was too late to turn around took away some of the pressure, but my instincts were still active.

I was startled when the door opened and a nurse walked into our room with two syringes on a tray. Adrian was asleep, but I had my eyes open. The nurse looked surprised to see me awake. She mumbled something I couldn't hear, then pointed to some socks on the floor and said, "Oh, um, pick those up, please."

That wasn't why she came into the room. I was sure she wanted to stick one of those needles into my skin, filling me up with designer chemicals. Who did she work for? Maybe she was supposed to deliver some gene-modified virus to alter my nervous system. To what end? No matter how I looked at it, there was nothing positive about this situation.

I stood and went to the door. I opened it slowly and looked down the long, neon-lit corridor. I couldn't see the nurse. Had she even been real? What does the word *real* even mean? As this question floated through my mind, I realized I no longer had a solid definition of reality.

I'd been taught that reality is a simulation within some hyper-intelligent mind, that it was supposed to be a field of infinite love or something like that. But I could see none of that love when I looked down the hall.

It was empty and cold, and behind each of its sealed metal doors was a patient struggling with their mind. Maybe some of them were being surprised by the evil nurse, too. Maybe they wouldn't even notice. The virus would corrupt their nervous system, and fear and paranoia would drag them to the bottom of a well of suffering. Maybe that was where I was now. Perhaps the evil nurse had already visited me, and this time she had been coming for Adrian. It didn't seem fair. None of it did. But what was I supposed to do about it?

I hadn't showered for a while, and cleaning my body felt like an attractive option. I stepped under the water and realized that the shampoo was suspicious. It smelled fine, but something about its consistency was weird. Maybe they hadn't given me the virus yet, and the shampoo was part of their new strategy. First, they tried with the sauce on the vegetables, then they tried with the nurse, and now they wanted to trick me with the shampoo. I decided not to use the shampoo.

My mind started spinning when I got out of the shower. There were so many possible threats. I needed someone to talk to, but Adrian was asleep or maybe in class. That was another weird thing. The only connection I had with him was outside of our bodies. I'd never really talked to him when he was in his body. I didn't know if he was having the same integration problems I was having, but he certainly didn't like to talk when we were in physical form.

He had said it was because of security reasons, which I guess made sense, but now I needed confirmation that what I was experiencing was real. Or maybe I needed proof that love was really beyond all of it. I thought for a moment and realized that I could never get confirmation within the illusion, because the thing I was trying to confirm existed beyond it. I had experienced many things beyond the illusion of form that showed me the enormous power of love. But down here, in my body, everything was dried up and cold. My joints ached, and my body was tight and full of anger, fear, and paranoia.

I was sick of dealing with this physical personality. I thought it through and decided to leave my body behind. I had lost interest in protecting my physical self. Who cares if the nurse shoots me up with some gene-modified virus? Maybe I'll just leave my body forever.

I closed my eyes and pulled my blanket over my head. I focused on the *Access* sign and landed in the classroom. The teacher was sitting in the corner, and there was another strange being giving a lecture. The being stopped whatever it was doing and waited for me to float into my seat. Instantly, I felt better. My worries and my paranoia were gone, and a friendly feeling of trust and belonging embraced me.

The being teaching us resembled a troll. It wore a crumpled fedora and had a long red beard. The first thing I thought was, *This being is a fool.* It made me laugh, and I knew that the creature had nothing against being a fool. That was the whole point. It was talking about not giving a shit about others' judgments.

It said in a raspy voice, "I picked these filthy lifetimes to embrace the filth." Then it laughed. Its laugh was very rich, and a couple of students were slapping their desks with their palms while the troll laughed. His energy was extraordinary and infectious; he seemed to invigorate the entire class. The atmosphere was like that of a sports bar.

He continued talking, "There are a million paths to the light. I have chosen the one that leads through the dirt. Look at me! I am a goddamn ugly fool!" He laughed again, and the whole class erupted. At this point, I couldn't resist either and began roaring with laughter, banging on the desk in front of me. There was just too much free-floating energy in the air. I had to express it as well, and it felt great.

"Listen," he said. He lowered his voice and continued. "Once upon a time there was a small family. Three children and a grandmother. It was cold outside, and the children were hungry . . ."

He told a story that had absolutely no point and no meaning, at least as far as I could tell. It was about the mundane existence of the small family he had described. I wondered what had happened to the parents, but apparently that was superfluous information. Instead, he told us how they took turns gathering firewood, and how the youngest girl got upset. At some point, the other children stopped going outside, and she was the only one who took care of the fire. But it was the way he told the story that fascinated me. He made the most quotidian details seem special and attention-grabbing.

Finally, after everyone had become completely absorbed in his story, he said, "Now you are present. How does it feel?"

I was caught off guard by the question. I had to shift my attention to reflecting on and wondering about how I felt. While I had been listening to him, I hadn't even been aware of my existence. During the telling, his story had been all that mattered.

No one answered the troll's question, so after a moment of silence, he said, "My story did not matter. What felt good was the fact that you were completely focused on one thing."

In a flash, the troll transformed into a glowing orb, and then reappeared as a monk, much taller and wrapped in a dark orange robe. He said, "I had this body a couple of centuries ago. I used it to explore the discipline of focus. As a monk, I learned to sit still and focus on the most mundane things. I have probably spent twenty thousand hours concentrating on my breathing. That sounds boring, right? Perhaps not much

118

more boring than the story I just told you. Things are only boring when you are not fully focused on them. It is all about focus!

"It does not matter what you focus on, but there is one distinction. If outside stimulus is what captures your attention, then you are dependent on entertainment. If you have found the fascination of the moment within yourself, you can go there anytime, no matter what's around you. This is what meditation does to you. You focus on your breath, on an image, on a mantra, or on the sensations of your body, and this mundane activity eventually captures all your attention. You become fully immersed in the present moment, and that is where you find your true self, but on the way there, your concept of self will be challenged.

"When you focus your mind on one thing, you will notice that all the psychological drives trying to find gratification are outside of yourself. If you just sit there, they will try to go into the past or the future to imagine things that entertain you. It is a chemical addiction. I explored this topic in another body."

He became a white orb once again and then reappeared as a woman wearing a lab coat.

The woman said, "I used this body to explore the topic from a scientific perspective. What I have found is that our neurological infrastructure develops patterns or relationships between the different aspects of the nervous system. Our awareness finds comfort in the familiarity of these relationships, even if they are not beneficial to our health. For example, a person who was raised by abusive parents, or a person who spent a significant amount of time in an abusive relationship, will become addicted to the stress hormones that those conflicts created. And when there are no physical conflicts, the person will be inclined to imagine stressful scenarios that will, in turn, signal the adrenal glands to release the stress hormones adrenaline and cortisol. These chemicals give the body a burst of energy upon which the person is dependent.

"This is not only the case with stress hormones. The same principle governs the mind and the body in subtler ways. If we spend a significant amount of time identifying with a particular self-image, we can become addicted to that image. A self-image, or a belief about one's self, is a neural network from the perspective of physical reality. If we continually think the same thoughts about ourselves, the connections within our brain that send signals to our body become strengthened. If we send our body the same chemical signals, our body and mind become dependent on that connection. In other words, we end up trying to recreate situations so that we can think about ourselves in the same way and send the same chemical messages to our body.

"We need this familiar neurological pattern to feel secure. Even if the pattern does not give us security, we still subconsciously seek out the familiar and fear the new. If you are used to being angry, you will try to find a way to stay angry, even if your circumstances improve. If you are an anxious person, you will seek out thoughts and experiences that will keep you in a familiar state of anxiety.

"You may ask why the human body has evolved such dysfunctional perception patterns. Well, the same mechanism can manifest as both beneficial and dysfunctional. Your body is a dynamic system of behavioral feedback loops, or habits. The key is to lift this system to its full potential and create positive habits, to find a positive resonance between your energy body and your physical body. If you constantly submit to the chemical needs of your body, your soul will become overpowered by physical and chemical processes.

"However, you can also use the willpower of your soul to change the biochemical and neurological habits of your physical body. For example, when you notice yourself getting angry at something, you can always choose to stop feeding the thought process that triggers the release of adrenaline. Your energy body has the power to override all your habits, but you must do it habitually. You can only change a habit by replacing it with another habit. Every time you notice that a pattern is controlling you, you must make a conscious choice to modify your pattern. This brings me back to the topic of focus."

She transformed into the body of the monk once again and continued. "You need the ability to focus if you want to confront your habits, and this is something that you have to practice. It does not matter how you practice focus, as long as you focus on something and resist all urges that try to distract you. You can stare at a fire, and if you do it with diligence and discipline, it will improve your ability to focus. Let's say you are staring at the fire and a thought pops in that says, 'Ah, these flames remind me of something.' If you follow that thought, you are no longer focused on the fire. Now you are thinking about the fire, but you are not focused on what the fire is. When you are fully focused on the fire, there are no thoughts, only fire. This brings me back to my story."

The monk became the troll, and with a raspy voice and a big grin, he picked up his ridiculous story where it had left off. "One day, the youngest daughter was sitting next to the fire. She was staring deep into the flames, thinking about the fact that the other two children hadn't gathered any firewood in days. This upset her very much, and she was consumed by anger and resentment. The grandmother came over and sat down next to her. She put her hand on the child's shoulder and said, 'My dear, you have gone outside and gathered firewood so that these flames can keep burning, but you cannot even enjoy them. Instead, you are dwelling on angry thoughts. Let them go and look at the flames.'

"The young girl listened to her grandmother and intensified her gaze. For one moment, the clouds of thought cleared away, and she saw the fire, bright and pure, burning in front of her."

The troll laughed and said, "Now, each of you, spend more time looking at the fire within yourself. Feel your breath, feel that you are alive, and make that the source of your joy. It doesn't matter what other people do or think. Stare at the fire within you."

He took several bows while the whole class applauded.

Our teacher stood and shook the troll's hand. He said, "Thank you so much for coming through!"

"Thank you so much for opening your class to the interdimensional community."

After returning to my body, I remained angry and confused, but I also realized a few things now. The things he/she/it said about habits and emotional addiction made a lot of sense.

I had spent a dozen years in misery and rage. Being homeless made it difficult to maintain a positive attitude, to say the least. The emotional patterns I had acquired were still within me, but now that my consciousness was on another level, I could no longer abide by these patterns.

The temptation to fall into anger and fear were constantly trying to grab my attention, screaming at me, "Be afraid! Worry about this! Get angry at that!" It was scary. I didn't trust anyone in the hospital. It was easy to forget about my fears when I wasn't in my body, but experiencing the frightening existence of a mental patient was challenging.

Adrian had already left. I got up and walked down the long corridor. I felt uneasy as I saw Agent 455 approaching me. I hoped he would just pass by, but he stopped right next to me. He said, "They are coming after you."

He didn't close his mouth when he finished the sentence. Instead, he exposed his rotten teeth and let out a high-pitched laugh that chilled my bones. I stared at him for a second and then kept walking. I got to the cafeteria, picked up the plate with my name on it, and sat down beside Adrian.

I took the cover off my plate, but this time the sauce had been poured over every bit of the meal. I looked at Adrian's plate. He had no sauce at all. What the hell was going on?

A nurse came over and took my tray. She replaced it with another one and said, "Here, eat this."

I uncovered the food, and there was no sauce anywhere. I smiled and thanked her. At that moment, I trusted the nurse, and a warm feeling flooded my entire body, relaxing my tense muscles. I ate gratefully. *What a healthy emotion*, I thought. *Much better than all the stress and anger that people are passing around here in the hospital.* I returned to my room with a full stomach, excited to leave my body again.

CHAPTER 16

I landed in the classroom. Dolster had once again invited a hyper-evolved alien being to present its ideas. This time it was an octopus-like creature that floated in front of the class. It was talking about the difference between form and spirit.

It explained, "We are all spirits, consciousnesses, glowing orbs, or whatever you want to call us. We travel between universes to collect diverse experiences. I had this body in another universe. It was difficult to transcend the cultural conditioning of this species. Like humans, many species get stuck in the beliefs of the small self, in the habitual ways of being. You believe that you are a physical being who is terrified of death. That is the core belief that keeps us stuck in form.

"It often takes hundreds of lifetimes until one masters the psychology of a physical being, but not because it requires that much experience. It takes so long because it requires a very specific circumstance. We need to get in touch with the teaching, and we need to be willing to apply the teaching. It is challenging to recognize the teaching as a tool to upgrade your being-ness. But some beings discover the teaching and take it to heart. They recognize it as a method to expand their consciousness, and a possibility to go beyond their beliefs.

"Belief is a tool that shapes your consciousness, but it never defines you. If you let it define you, you must go through the process of living out the ideas that you created for yourself. The teaching tells you that you don't have to waste entire lifetimes on self-images that your social environment has made you believe. The teaching says that you are always more than what you believe, which is entirely logical but difficult to understand. If you are the one thinking a thought that you believe, then your thought is a consequence of you. You create your thoughts; therefore, your thoughts can never define you.

"Many beings identify with their creations. We get distracted by all the things we have believed ourselves to be, and we prevent ourselves from seeing who we are. But belief is a creative act and not something that defines you or others. You might ask, 'So what are we then?' The answer is that we are that which defines; we are not the definition."

At that moment the classroom disappeared. I fell through the floor. It was nothing like the other times I had left the classroom. I felt a drunken dizziness as I came back into my body. I felt nauseous. I could barely move.

I opened my eyes slowly and saw that I was hooked up to an IV. A guard and a nurse stood beside me. When my eyes met theirs, the nurse took a step forward and did something to the IV. My vision became even blurrier, and I gradually faded into complete darkness.

I don't know how long I was unconscious. When I awoke, I was alone in an unfamiliar white room. I closed my eyes again and discovered that I could no longer see the link to the classroom nor the crash report. My first thought was that PsyOp had fired me and I was now just a mental patient.

After some time, a nurse holding a clipboard entered the room. She asked, "Greg, how are you feeling?"

I tried to speak, but my mouth and tongue would not move as I intended. Instead, I produced incomprehensible sounds. The nurse checked off something on her clipboard and left the room. Where was I? What was happening to me?

The next time a nurse came in—a different one this time—I asked her, "What's going on?"

She looked at me indifferently and checked off something on her clipboard. The days that followed were a blur. The next thing I remember vividly is meeting Dr. Rab.

Dr. Rab was a psychiatrist. I wasn't sure what decisions had been made in the upper levels of the hospital organization, but I had been transferred to a single room, and I was required to see him.

Dr. Rab's eyes were puffy, and his chin was swallowed up by extra skin. He spoke fast and often tripped over his own words. I was sitting across from him, and he asked, "Do you know where you are?"

I had barely thought about the location of my body and had forgotten where I was. I knew I was in some hospital, but I didn't know the name. I said, "I'm in the hospital."

Dr. Rab said, "You are at Kings County Hospital. Do you know why you are here?"

"I'm paid to be here."

"No, you started a fight in the cafeteria while you were in prison."

"Yeah, but I only did that because it was a prerequisite of my job offer."

"Who offered you a job?"

"Jeff was his name."

"Where did you meet Jeff?"

"I left my body and met him in a parallel reality."

Dr. Rab scribbled something on his notepad. Then he asked, "Do you see Jeff now?"

"No, I haven't seen him since."

"Have you had any other hallucinations?"

"They were not hallucinations!"

126

"Hallucinations always seem real to the people having them. You were the only person who could see Jeff, right?"

"Yeah, but that's because we were sharing another . . ." I heard my own words and stopped. I felt unsure. Was I crazy?

Dr. Rab saw my confusion and smiled. "Schizophrenia is a tough illness to deal with. Fortunately, we have medications that work very well. I will prescribe you 20 milligrams of Zyprexa."

"I don't think I need medication. The stuff I was taking before was only so I could leave my body more easily."

"Your file says that you were taking sleeping pills, but you have been diagnosed with schizophrenia and are legally required to take Zyprexa. I don't know why they were giving you sleeping pills. We don't want there to be another invisible Jeff who tells you to harm others. You don't want that either."

I began to doubt myself even more. Maybe I really was sick. I certainly felt sick. My stomach and chest hurt, and it was a pain I knew well. Had I escaped into a fantasy world to avoid the pain?

I agreed, "Okay, I guess I'll take it, then."

"Yes, it will help you go on with your life. I mean, do you want to stay in this hospital for the rest of your life?"

"No, I don't, but I thought I had to finish my contract."

"What contract?"

"The contract I signed with Jeff."

"Do you have this contract?"

"No, it was in another reality."

"You mean it was part of a hallucination?"

"I guess . . ." This conversation was making me feel very ill. Dr. Rab was slowly stripping away my confidence and my ability to decide what was real and unreal. Only a few days earlier, I had thought I could leave my body, and I had a broader understanding of what creates the problems of human existence.

Accepting that I was crazy was difficult. It made me feel weak and incompetent, and worst of all, it made me feel like I could not trust myself.

Dr. Rab was telling me that the experience of other realities was a symptom of a mental illness. He studied psychiatry, and I thought he probably knew more than I did. How could I trust myself when the things I believed to be true were symptoms of mental illness? My entire body was filled with shame. I could barely breathe.

Dr. Rab smiled. He saw that my confidence was crumbling, and he seemed pleased that I was finally beginning to accept my illness. He said, "Accepting that you are sick is the first step to recovery. Your hallucinations have harmed you and other people. Schizophrenia is a serious illness, but the medication I have prescribed will take care of the symptoms. Just make sure you take them."

CHAPTER 17

When I left Dr. Rab's office my head was hanging low. I walked down the long corridor connecting the different parts of the facility, and my gaze was fixed on my own shadow. I watched it change as I passed under the different lights mounted on the ceiling. I noticed a window. Snow fell outside. I looked through the glass and could see a barren tree in front of a small brick house. I hadn't thought about the outside world in weeks, or maybe even months. I hadn't even realized that it was winter.

The sidewalk was covered in snow, and I remembered how my mom and I used to go on walks through the snow. She always made sure that I was wearing warm enough clothes before she let me play in the snow. As I looked out the window, with my forehead pressed against the glass, I realized that I wanted to live a life. I didn't just want to dream my life away and vegetate in the hospital.

I was still confused about what was real or unreal, what was sick or healthy, but instead of dwelling on these questions, I wanted to simplify my life. Living on the streets had only made my life more complicated. I ended up in a mental hospital, living in a fantasy world for months. If this was where my path had led me, I wanted to try a different path.

I looked at the clean white snow, and I remembered my mother's caring smile. She would have wanted me to take care of myself. I owed it to her to put on some normal, warm clothes in place of the blue jumpsuit I wore now, and to have a roof over my head that wasn't part of a hospital. I wanted to sit on a couch, watch a movie, and eat hot soup. That would be a good start.

I thought I might even try to go back to school, get a degree or something. I wondered if Harvard would take me back. Or maybe I could learn to play an instrument. That would be fun.

Later that night, as I lay in bed and tried to fall asleep, I realized I had forgotten how. I hadn't slept in months. I was always awake in one reality or another. How could I fall asleep?

As I pondered this problem, a voice said, "Imagine a river far below your bed, and then jump into that river."

The voice startled me. I now accepted that this kind of stuff was a symptom of my illness. I opened my eyes and felt a burst of fear spread through my body. *Damn, I'm still hearing voices*, I thought.

The voice said, "Crazy is an illusion, but I will let you figure it out for yourself. I will leave you alone now."

I knew it was Umbumi's voice, but I didn't want to pronounce his name. There was a tiny bit of curiosity beneath my fear, but my medicated brain told me that it could be dangerous to follow my curiosity.

In any case, that didn't solve my predicament. I had forgotten how to fall asleep. That couldn't be normal. Maybe I was special? I feared that thought too.

These ideas bounced back and forth in my brain, until I finally decided to get up and ask a nurse for sleeping pills. It was late at night, but other patients were still awake. Some were walking back and forth, while others sat on chairs in a common area.

I realized that I didn't know anything about them. I didn't recognize a single person. I had lived in this hospital for months, but I had used it as a parking garage. I had left my body here and gone elsewhere.

I thought about Adrian and Joey. Where were they? Were they real? Did I really have a friend named

Adrian? But those thoughts drifted away, and I was left with the kind of uneasy feeling you get when your best friend steals a lot of money from you. I had the aftertaste of betrayal in my mouth, and I wanted to spit it out. I wanted to vomit, but I was ashamed of myself and thought I shouldn't vomit on the floor.

I swallowed my emotions and tried to contain myself. *That's normal,* I thought. *I must be normal now. Normal people control their emotions. That's how it's supposed to be. And I need to look better. I need better clothes, and I should be driving a nice car when I get out of the hospital.*

I found a nurse and asked her for some sleeping pills. She gave them to me, along with something to calm me down. She handed me a small paper cup of grape juice. I swallowed both pills and thanked her. *I am polite,* I thought. *I am a polite man.*

I walked back to my room and laid my body on the mattress. In the past, this would have excited me because it meant I was about to go on an adventure, but now I was stuck with my terrible feelings and thoughts. Why did I need these terrible feelings and thoughts?

I heard a different voice this time. "To transform them." I wasn't going to engage with the voices anymore, so I ignored this one as well. I decided to stop asking questions. Soon the medications kicked in, and I drifted into a strange sleep.

I woke the next day and felt drowsy. I left my new room, which was on the other side of the facility from my old room, and I walked along the corridor to the cafeteria.

I had eaten in the cafeteria countless times, but I had never really talked to anyone. I always thought of eating as something I wanted to get over with as quickly as possible. Being awake was a burden, but now it was all I had. I didn't even remember my dreams. Maybe being here with the other patients was better than being alone in my bed.

I looked at a young woman sitting across from me. I was startled to see that it was Anna.

I didn't know what to say at first, but then I asked her in a soft voice, "Am I hallucinating?"

She laughed. "You are always hallucinating, unless you are one with all that is. I guess what you want to know is if other people can see me too. That depends on how sensitive they are. But I am here for you. What is important is that you can see and hear me clearly."

She looked at me with a loving smile and said, "Greg, don't believe them. Stay true to yourself, but play along with them so they let you out of here. Don't believe them; just play along with their game. Oh, I am crazy. Oh, she is crazy. Oh, we are all crazy. That's the game they play here. But what is really crazy? What is crazy, Greg? What is it?"

Anna's voice had begun to rise, and her intensity was a bit intimidating.

"Um . . . I don't know . . . uh," I stammered.

"Why do you identify with something that has no concrete meaning to you? What are you identifying with?" She was looking directly at me, her eyes piercing the fog that had clouded my heart.

Suddenly, I began to see more clearly, and together we said, "Fear!"

"Yes, Greg. If you identify as sick, you are identifying with fear. If you are identifying with crazy, you are trapped in the illusory search for what is normal. Does normal exist, Greg? Does it exist?"

Her energy was very confrontational. I could see a warrior shooting arrows through her dark eyes, and I knew that it was the kind of warrior I would like to be. These days of meaningless confusion had shown me where the search for normal was leading, and it was definitely not where I wanted to be.

I saw a pale man sitting in a corner of the cafeteria. He looked directly at me, and as our eyes met, I thought, *Maybe it's not the search for normal that was the problem. Maybe the problem was that I had actually gone crazy.*

Anna was still looking at me, but she noticed that our connection was broken. She asked, "What was that? What did you just think?"

I was confused. I looked back at the pale man in the corner and realized that he was a security guard. His eyes seemed to penetrate my mind, and I no longer thought it safe to tell Anna about my own thoughts. Maybe it was not even safe to think these kinds of thoughts.

She was still looking at me with a loving-but-forceful gaze. She said, "Greg, don't let fear get to you. You have to love the shit out of all fear. Love it to death, Greg. Love it!"

Although what she said sounded paradoxical, it made sense to me. It struck a chord deep within me, and the vibration shook my whole body. But there were mufflers attached to my bones that did not like the song she tried to get me to sing.

She said, "Sing the song, Greg! Sing it!"

I looked at her, and for a second, her face was purple and I saw Armassa. But then her face morphed back to the one I knew as Anna.

"Anna," I said. "Who are you?"

With a soft voice, she answered, "I am the song you are trying to sing." She looked deep into my eyes and touched my hand softly. "Greg, I am the song you are trying to sing. I am here to help you sing it. We are with you."

As she said this, I thought I saw my mother. I felt my mother's love in her voice. A tear dripped down my cheek, and I felt another string getting plucked. It echoed through my flesh, and a purple flower began to sprout. It grew out of my chest and straight across the room like a vine on a string. When it reached the pale man in the corner, he began to smile. The flower dissolved into purple light, and fog settled over the entire room.

For a second, I thought, *Great, now I'm hallucinating without leaving my body.*

But Anna interrupted my thought. She said, "Yes, Greg, everything is a hallucination. That is the song. That is it. Form isn't real. It is a visual metaphor for the vibrations you and others create. I did not see the flower that grew out of your chest, but I heard it, smelled it, felt it. It's the song that counts, not the ears that listen to it. Do you understand, Greg? Do you understand me?"

What she said made absolutely no sense, but I fully understood her. It resonated with a deep part of me, the part of me that once was a medicine woman, the part of me that spoke with the fire.

She took my other hand and pulled me closer. I was very close to her face, and her lips were inches away from mine. I could feel her breath, and suddenly our lips touched. In the corner of my eye, I could see the security guard approaching. He was looking right at us, and his face bore an expression of heartless authority. It was clear that kissing in the cafeteria was not permitted.

I pulled back, but Anna said, "No, just kiss me a bit more strongly." I understood what she meant, so I kissed her not just with my lips, but with all my heart. I remembered what I had learned with the ancestors, and

I let myself fall into the snake pit, through the fear and pain, and into trust.

I heard the ancestors drumming and singing, and Anna's lips were pulsating to the beat. The song rippled outward, and I saw that the security guard had stopped midway to us and pulled out his phone. He plugged in his headphones, listened for a second, and said, "That is a damn good song."

Anna looked at me as if she had observed the whole thing through the back of her head and said, "Synchronicities occur when you sing your song. Others then sing their own songs, or at least listen to a song!" She laughed.

A part of me wanted to ask how this had just happened. Why did the security guard change his mind and listen to a song instead of interrupting us? But another part knew the answer.

The answer was not conceptual. It was right there in the room, and we were there too. It was easy to recognize that. We were together, the question and the answer. So in agreement with this truth, we kept kissing, and Anna asked me if I would like to come to her room.

"Your room?" I asked. "Why do you have a room here?"

"Because we need a room."

I laughed, realizing that it was pointless to try to find the consistent reality I once knew. "Okay," I said.

We walked along the corridor and watched the light reflecting on the floor. She opened a white door not far from my room. Her bed was much bigger, and a vase of flowers sat on her desk. I hadn't seen flowers since my time with the ancestors. As my gaze absorbed their colors, I realized that I had never seen flowers with my body, or at least I had never seen them like I could see them now.

I walked closer to the vase and touched the flowers' delicate petals. I felt the vibrational patterns that these flowers emanated and recognized them as honest and true. I turned to Anna and said, "I'm so happy to see flowers. How did you get them?"

"It is not important. Come into my arms!" She was lying on her bed and had begun to undress. I walked towards her and placed my hands on her thighs. I began to massage her body. I enjoyed the anticipation. It felt like a tingling river of fireworks. I surrendered to the feeling and found myself in an ecstatic current of love. It washed me to several beaches, each one full of different sensations and pleasures.

Anna was moaning, and I was drenched in sweat. She whispered into my ear, "Thank you."

I whispered back, "Thank you."

She said, "We need a word for a mutual thank you."

I suggested, "Thank us?" We both laughed.

I left Anna's room, and as I closed her door, I saw the door change color and shrink. I opened it back up and saw that I had walked out of the janitor's closet. I don't know how connected this experience was with the consistent reality we all agree exists, or if there was such a thing as an objective reality. What mattered was how this experience affected me. My head felt clear, and my heart felt wide open.

Before I saw Anna, fear had been getting to me. I realized that Dr. Rab had actually been unhelpful. I had given him way too much power, and I had believed him. He was good at convincing people. He should have become a lawyer, but here he was convincing mental patients that they had gone crazy, which wasn't really that hard. After all, they were in a mental hospital, and they were wearing blue jumpsuits. Anyone locked in a cell here would begin to doubt their own sanity.

It was difficult to stay confident about your own truth when the doctors looked at you with pity, while silently congratulating themselves that they had won another case. I was in the middle of a twisted game, and the rules were no longer clear, but Anna had helped me make my own rules. She never told me to make my own rules, but the twinkle in her eyes showed me that it could be done.

I realized that I should not tell Dr. Rab about any experience that he would consider abnormal. I needed to follow a new set of rules for the game. There was Dr. Rab, who perceived reality to be just what the five senses could detect, and it was his job to medicate those who experienced a broader reality. Then there were the patients, who experienced a larger reality but hadn't fully integrated their experiences, and they were therefore easily influenced.

The most difficult part of the game was ignoring Dr. Rab when he told you that you were mentally ill. If you believed him, he would make you afraid of your own experiences.

I began to understand that fear was driving Dr. Rab, and that fear was using him to drive more fear into his patients. I guess the goal of this fear was to conceal the truth and to contain paranormal experiences. The lid of the container was the fear of insanity.

CHAPTER 18

I was beginning to understand what was going on, and I was filled with rage. How many patients were out there taking medications for the rest of their lives, just because they were afraid of what they had experienced?

I could see how it would be easier to forget about these intense experiences. I didn't want to think about them, either. I still felt nauseous about some of the things I had witnessed. It was tempting to write them off as hallucinations, take medication, sit on a couch, and watch TV. But there was another part of me that refused that option.

I wanted to stamp my feet and throw furniture, but I didn't do that. I chose to contain my rage, smile at Dr. Rab, and tell him to go fuck himself so politely that he wouldn't even notice.

So I said, "No, Doctor. I don't have hallucinations anymore."

As I spoke, I watched a black cloud of smoke circle his head. It was filled with morphing faces that looked like they were smiling, but their teeth were ready to rip you into pieces. Anna had opened a door for me, and other realities were once again as real as everything else.

There was no undoing what I had learned. The more time I spent in my body, the more the things I had experienced outside of it merged with my physical reality. I said, "I'm feeling a lot better. How are you feeling?"

I was looking a bit past the doctor's eyes and addressing the tortured faces wrapped around his head. He twitched a little, and his eyes opened and closed frantically until he managed to hold on to a thought that offered him security. He clearly did not want to face his own fear, and he found comfort in the idea that he was the doctor and I was the patient. He liked the illusion of control that this status provided.

He said, "Don't worry about me. I am here to help you get better."

He said it with such conviction that I doubted myself for a second. Was I really crazy? I saw all sorts of things, and I could hear things too. The nasty entities sucking the juices out of Dr. Rab's brain were now staring at me intently. One even reached over to see if it could anchor itself in my doubt, but there wasn't enough fear for that. It slipped right off.

I remembered how these nasty fuckers operated. I remembered the game they played. Dr. Rab had made me doubt my position, but that didn't mean I was powerless to defend myself. I knew who I used to be. I remembered the life of a medicine woman. I remembered healing people through vibrations, and in my head, I began to hear the drumming of the ancestor tree. I began to feel the immense power stored in my Akalele.

Wordlessly, I danced out of my head. I danced through the air. I danced right through Dr. Rab's head. I saw the jungle reclaim its territory as flowers began growing from his ears. I saw the black smoke around his head as soil. I imagined performing one of Arilla's planting rituals. I kissed his fears like Arilla used to kiss the soil that had never seen the sun. With my love, I was planting seeds into Dr. Rab's vibration, and I was watching them grow to the sound of the drums.

Dr. Rab blinked frantically, and his body trembled while I smiled at him. For a few seconds, he had fallen under the spell of the dance, and the cells in his body were dancing—whether he liked it or not. But he shook himself loose and grabbed for his pen. His fingers struggled to get it under control. He looked at me, puzzled, and said, "What were you saying?"

"I didn't say anything. I was just sitting here."

He began writing on his notepad, but he didn't add any new information. He retraced the outlines of the date and other information that he had already written.

"Okay, Greg. I am glad you are doing better, I will talk to you next Wednesday." He tried to seem sure of himself, but he was clearly losing the battle. I didn't believe him one bit, and I knew that my belief was now strong enough to withstand his presence. I wanted to laugh when I left his office, but my smile was interrupted by an unexpected encounter.

Umbumi was standing in the hallway. His body was slightly transparent, and he looked earnest.

"Greg," Umbumi said. "When you use your healing power against someone's will, it becomes dark magic. It corrupts the spirit of our tribe. We want to teach you how to deal with Dr. Rab without fighting against him. But we can't have you standing here talking to thin air. You need to seem normal to everyone in the hospital, so go to your room and close the door."

I noticed that a nurse with a clipboard was already looking at me. I smiled at her and walked to my cell. Umbumi was floating next to me, but I pretended that he was not there until I sat down on my bed.

"Don't speak to me," he said. "We can communicate through thought. You don't want a nurse catching you in conversation with yourself.

"I have come to you because we noticed that you are beginning to integrate our wisdom. The things your Akalele has learned are beginning to rewire your body. This means that some of your powers are now beginning to become accessible through the personality of Greg. But Greg still has a lot of hate and anger inside of him, and it could be dangerous if Greg's hate mixes with the wisdom of the healer you have been in our tribe. You can use your power, but you must always use it with understanding and compassion for others. This means that you cannot use our dance for a battle you are fighting. You can only use our dance when you understand that there is no battle to be fought.

"When you directed your energy towards Dr. Rab, you felt proud that you had dominated the interaction. Pride is poison. You only cause more pain through this mindset. You can use our dance, but only if you understand Dr. Rab's pain. Then you can help him out of it. But before you can understand Dr. Rab, you must forgive yourself for everything you have done, throughout all times. Are you ready to go on a little journey?"

I said "yes" without opening my mouth.

My vision blurred, and suddenly I saw myself climbing into a cave. All sorts of grotesque faces hung from the walls. It smelled like rotten flesh, and bones were scattered across the floor.

Gradually, the vision increased in vividness until it was all I experienced. Umbumi's voice had faded away, and it felt like a massive iron door had shut behind me. I was alone in a dark cave.

A cold feeling rippled down my spine. My chest tightened, and a dull pain spread through my body. I began to hear the whispers of hopelessness. The cave walls emitted a dim glow, and the floor was scattered with skeletons, each seeming to possess a strange vitality.

My eyes met the empty sockets of a human skull, and I heard a greeting in my mind. It was a strange word that I didn't recognize, but the intention was something like, "Hello, you are now here as well, and you also deserve to die."

Although it was only one short word, it was immediately clear to me that this skeleton wanted me as dead as it was. I looked at my feet and was startled to see maggots all over the floor. I jumped backward and almost fell when I landed on a pile of bones.

My reaction seemed to amuse the skull. I heard a loud laugh reverberate through the cave, and the skull lit up from within. Black smoke oozed from its eye sockets, and soon the smoke took on a more solid form. A face emerged. It was my face, deformed and perverted like an evil caricature. It was the shadow-being in its purest form.

"I am your dark self," it said. As it spoke, I felt another wave of fear. This seemed to amuse it. "I am the one you have been running from. I am your dark self, and now you finally have no place left to run."

It grew larger and began to take on a more distinct form. Some parts of its body retained rotten flesh, while others lacked any flesh at all and revealed its bones.

I was terrified. I tried visualizing my body at the hospital, but whether my eyes were open or closed made no difference. All I saw was the horrible being looking at me with a foul grin. I tried visualizing Umbumi, but the creature extended its thin arms and yanked the vision right out of my skull. I watched the image disappear into its hands.

The creature laughed. "If you think you can leave, think again!" I tried to think, but I could not. All I experienced was the terrible existence of this being and my resistance to it.

It felt as if I was on a leash that was sending electric shocks through my whole body. I was trapped by an evil version of myself and could not move. For what could have been hours, I was paralyzed by an overwhelming fear. I had lost my sense of time.

After a hopeless mental struggle, I began accepting my situation. Gradually, my resistance faded.

It whispered, "I am your dark self . . . I am your dark self . . . I am your dark self . . ."

It was still scary, but I no longer minded it as much. I had resisted as strongly as I could, but I didn't have much energy left.

With my new attitude, I began perceiving a stillness in the cave that was only occasionally broken by the sound of water dripping from stalactites. They had probably been dripping the whole time, but fear had consumed my attention and shrouded my perception. Now I could hear clearly how the water landed on stone surfaces and sent gentle ripples of sound through the cave.

It felt like I had awakened from a nightmare, but my surroundings were the same. The shadow still stood before me, grinning with my own deformed face, but now I saw a new element in it. I was calm enough to look through its terrifying appearance, and I felt sadness and guilt, like a child who blamed himself for the death of his parents.

The shadow-being began to dissolve back into black smoke, and within the smoke, I saw a door floating in midair. As soon as I looked at the door, the knob turned, and the door opened. I was sucked into a dark tunnel. Its walls were covered with memories. They were like movies playing beside each other on irregularly shaped screens.

On one big screen, I saw my mother's gravestone. My five-year-old self knelt next to it, crying, "Mommy! Mommy, please come back! Why don't you come back? I'm a good boy. Please, Mommy!"

Intense shivers traveled through my body as I understood that I had pushed away a part of me, the part

143

that believed I was responsible for my parents' deaths. Because I withheld love and truth from it, it had become my shadow. I had pushed it away and never allowed it to heal. It had sabotaged my life because it wanted me to pay attention to it. Now love and understanding filled my heart.

I could hear Umbumi's voice. He was speaking in a foreign language, but his words had a powerful effect on me. They nurtured the seed of forgiveness within me, and I could feel a warm tingling expanding my heart, welcoming the shadow-being with love and truth. A sense of wholeness spread through my body, and I returned to the hospital bed with Umbumi hovering above me. He moved his hands like the medicine people of the ancestor tribe used to do.

Umbumi said, "We all have dwelled in darkness. Maybe you can understand now what Dr. Rab is going through. Let me show you."

Visions flooded my mind. I could see Dr. Rab sitting in front of a television while he stuffed fried chicken into his mouth. I could feel his mind racing, and the empty feeling inside him. He held the box of fried chicken like it was his last hope, and I felt sad. I felt Dr. Rab's pain and desperation. I saw now that the experience he had with me had contributed to his confusion and made him resent his job even more.

The vision faded away, and Umbumi said, "Dr. Rab needs love. He has no love for himself, and he has no love for his job. He needs love."

Umbumi faded away, and I was left with my thoughts and emotions. I wanted to cry. It was apparent that there was a big misunderstanding between the light and the dark. I was no longer afraid of the evil wills of others. On a deeper level, I understood the pain of those who chose to hurt others. I had accepted the skeleton in

144

the cave as part of myself, and this increased my ability to feel compassion.

CHAPTER 19

One night, as I was dozing off, I felt my body shake. I
heard the familiar popping sound, felt a pulling in my
chest, and found myself back in the classroom. A few
other students were there, but I recognized none of
them. Adrian wasn't there either. It seemed like a
different class, but Dolster was teaching it.

He greeted me. "Welcome, Greg."

He had never called me by my real name, and it
felt good to hear him say it out loud.

He continued, "Everyone in this class has
already met their dark self and has forgiven themselves.
We'll be working on sharing this forgiveness with
others. It's a lifelong journey. We can always dive
deeper into our self and acquire new levels of
forgiveness and love. But all of you have reached a
point where you can help others with their fears. You
have faced the fear within you, you have met your
ugliest selves, and you have accepted them. You can
now help others do the same."

As he said this, he pulled one of the long, ferret-
like creatures from his mouth. It was enveloped by
black smoke that dripped from his chin like liquid
nitrogen. The creature emitted quiet, high-pitched
screams as Dolster cradled it gently in his hands.

He kissed it tenderly, and the creature seemed to
be slowly calming down. After a moment, it dissolved
into golden mist.

"Love your fear," Dolster said in a breathy
voice. Then he looked at us and continued, "My friends,
love your fear with all your heart. You could never be
who you are now if you had not experienced your fears.
Darkness is not scary. Darkness is rich and beautiful,
full of power, full of passion, just waiting to be
liberated.

"You have already liberated many aspects of yourself. Now let's go kiss the fear of others. Let's go sing songs for them. You won't get paid for this work, but I can see that the love in your hearts desires liberation for all."

He smiled at us brightly, a gentle glow surrounding his face. Then he said, "I love you, my dear students." He paused before going on. "Here's what we are going to do. Just like you used to, you will find people and influence them, but instead of having specific results in mind, we'll simply raise each person's vibration. We'll be there with them, maybe singing them a song, or maybe holding their hand. They won't be able to see us or hear us since we're still working on a parallel reality, but our intentions will influence them. They will feel our intentions and our love. It will help them align with a higher vibration, and hopefully find peace and joy within their heart.

"This is how they will contribute to the new networks. Once they hold a vibration of love, they will instantly share their consciousness with all beings that also hold that vibration. So one by one, we will begin to anchor this higher vibration here on Earth. It's great fun, and the future is totally uncertain and limitless. We don't know what people will do with their expanded states of consciousness, but we know that it will be lovely."

He flashed us another one of his bright smiles, and I noticed that he had developed totally different facial features. He reminded me a lot of Umbumi. Dolster used to have the empty look of death in his eyes, but now there was a sparkle, like morning sun reflecting off the still water of a forest pond. He radiated warmth and compassion. He didn't judge his own fear anymore. Even when he pulled rotten creatures out of himself, he maintained a calmness in

147

his eyes and often said, "I know what I have done, I know what I have been, I know who I am now. I am here. I am here. I am here."

He seemed to have accepted the many faces he has worn and was no longer ashamed of his evil past. He held his fear in his hands, kissed it with tender forgiveness, and claimed his eternal self for the purpose of benefiting all. He was beginning to radiate the kind of energy that I knew only from the glowing orbs or the ancestors. Occasionally, his body began glowing so brightly that I could barely see his physical outline. At one point, he was radiating a purple light, and after it settled, Umbumi stood in front of us.

Umbumi smiled directly at me and said, "Mr. Dolster and I are one and the same multidimensional being."

He continued, "Greg, you have helped me remember. You carry the vibration of the ancestors with you. You have built the bridge."

This surprised me so much that I fell through the floor and woke up startled in my hospital bed.

I stared at the wall for a while, saying to myself, "Dolster was a part of Umbumi . . . Umbumi was a part of Dolster . . ."

It hurt to give up on the idea of individual personalities and accept the fluidity of identity, but I could feel a buzzing energy that seemed to be helping me with this process. With my eyes closed, I saw a white circle extending around my body. In the middle of the circle was something like a spinning tornado. Its tip descended and touched me between my eyes. Like a gentle tattoo needle, it moved around and carved geometric patterns into my forehead. Then it traveled down to my heart and did the same thing. This went on for a while, and it felt like something within in me was getting synchronized. When I opened my eyes again, I felt very peaceful. But then I began to think about Adrian. I wondered what could have happened to him. Why wasn't he in the new class? After all, he was the one who suggested that I should work for the other side. I couldn't imagine that he would have chosen to stay with PsyOp and believe his fears.

The door opened, and a nurse entered. She was carrying a tray with my medications and some grape juice. I took my medications and thanked her. When she left, I spat them back out.

The next time I landed in the classroom, Umbumi/Dolster was present as a glowing orb. He had no face, but he radiated a familiar and pleasant energy. He was teaching us how to share forgiveness with others. During the class, he occasionally morphed back to either Umbumi or Dolster, shifting freely between the two corporeal forms depending on which language he used. Sometimes he used the technical vocabulary of PsyOp and spoke as Dolster, other times he spoke more poetically and took on the shape of Umbumi.

After the class, I asked him where Adrian was. He became Umbumi and looked at me thoughtfully. Then he answered, "Adrian chose a very difficult path. His body is in a coma, and his Akalele is living another life. He will need several months of Earth time to finish the life he chose."

"What kind of life did he choose?"

Umbumi paused before saying, "He incarnated into one of the lower realms. He will have to face the constant threat of death."

"Why would he do that?"

"Adrian wanted to strengthen his will and liberate the beings trapped in the lower realms. Don't worry about him for now. He has made a courageous and selfless choice. In time, you may be required to help him remember who he is."

149

When I returned to my body, I felt sad and confused. Adrian had become a good friend, and I missed him.

I went alone to the cafeteria, which was now on the other side of the hallway from where I remembered it being. I wondered who had moved me while I was unconscious. But I wouldn't allow myself to get paranoid about it. The things I had been taught were beginning to seep into my body. I was feeling better, but at the same time, my nonphysical and physical realities were no longer completely separate.

CHAPTER 20

The next time I saw Dr. Rab, my mind flooded with visions. I could see what he was striving for, how he spent his free time, and all his fears and concerns. His private life was not hidden from me; it was like I could read his mind.

He spent most of his time thinking about which brands of medication to prescribe. Some brands offered him paid trips to conferences in Hawaii and the Bahamas. Based on my visions, these were more like paid vacations for the doctors who met their prescription quotas. He spent a lot of time thinking about these conferences, because some of them also had shuttle buses to strip clubs.

The game Dr. Rab played seemed twisted, and it certainly challenged my new-found acceptance. Feeling love for such a scumbag was difficult, but I knew that, deep down, he was a lost soul trapped by fear and delusion and protected by arrogance and malicious intentions. He was a skeleton in a deep, dark cave, but he was afraid to look at himself, to hold the skeleton and warm its bones. Instead, he was looking for protection by pretending to be a rich and powerful figure.

I sat down before Dr. Rab and looked him in the eyes. I focused on the love buried underneath his desperation, underneath his evil will, underneath his fear. He himself had forgotten about this love and was more concerned with the maintenance of his shell, his false sense of control. He wanted his colleagues to envy him; he wanted to be the one who throws $100 bills at the strippers in the club.

Some pharmaceutical companies offered him huge bonuses, and he needed those bonuses to maintain his lifestyle. He had been sucked into a trap and was digging himself deeper and deeper into the quicksand without realizing it. I knew the feeling. I saw him as an explorer who had fallen off the path and was now flailing his arms while seemingly solid ground melted beneath his feet. I genuinely wanted to help him, to extend my arm and pull him out.

I said, "Dr. Rab, I want to help you."

I really meant it, and a part of him must have recognized that because my gesture visibly disturbed him. As he struggled to find an appropriate response, his face twitched, and his words stuck in his throat.

I wanted to reach into his mouth and pull out the words. I wanted to be his savior. I extended my arm, but right before I touched Dr. Rab, Umbumi appeared next to him. I pulled my hand back. Umbumi shook his head in amusement.

"Compassion is a feeling," he said. "It is an energy. It is enough for you to hold that energy. If you make it too personal, you will end up convincing yourself that you are some type of savior. Hold the energy and remove yourself. It is not about you, and it is not about you finding an immediate solution to another's suffering. If you truly understand their suffering, you also understand their actions, and this understanding automatically invites them to free themselves."

Dr. Rab seemed to have regained his sense of confidence. He barked at me, "What are you looking at?"

I realized that I couldn't tell Dr. Rab about the larger reality. I had to try to appear sane so that he would allow me to leave the hospital.

I had the feeling that a lot of patients made the mistake of telling their psychiatrists what was happening. Well, maybe there were some psychiatrists who actually understood themselves, but these prescription fanatics in the larger facilities had no real understanding of mental illness. They were middlemen between the drug companies and the involuntary consumers. Any behavior they didn't understand was an opportunity to bring themselves closer to their next vacation.

I snapped back to Dr. Rab's reality and said that I was just a little tired. To sell it, I pretended to yawn, but it didn't really work. He looked at me with suspicion. He still seemed a little startled and glared at me intently, determined to find another symptom, another way to protect his superiority.

I said, "Don't worry about me, Doctor. I'm feeling a lot better. Things are pretty much back to normal."

As I said this, I saw two agents swirling above him. A focus aligner had also appeared and was trying to attach itself to his forehead. I could hear their orders. They wanted him to prescribe medications that would prevent me from anchoring to the new vibration.

I could have retreated into fear, but instead, I visualized a glowing orb. I put love and compassion into that orb, and with imaginary hands, placed it right above Dr. Rab's head. I heard a pop, and the agents disappeared. I chuckled a little bit.

Still suspicious, Dr. Rab looked at me and said, "What are you laughing about? Do you hear voices?"

"Yes," I said. "I hear your voice. You have a lovely voice."

I chuckled again, and this time I could feel him align with my vibration. He also laughed slightly. My joke was not that funny, but he must have felt the shift in energy when the agents left. It's easier to laugh when they aren't around.

I didn't know what the fear-based networks were like these days. They must have decided to deny me access; my vibration apparently wasn't workable anymore.

For the first time, Dr. Rab gave me a real smile. He had smiled before, or at least lifted his cheeks and exposed his teeth, but I had never considered those facial expressions to be genuine. This time, though, there was something that really amused him. He said, "Do you know the Frankers?"

I shook my head.

"Well, you remind me of one of the characters from that show." And he began telling me about a cartoon character he had loved as a kid. He told me the whole story of an entire episode, until he realized we had gone over our allotted time.

That night, I was in class again. We were now working with people all around the world. Dolster was taking us on a lot of missions to help others become the truest expressions of themselves.

During one mission, Umbumi took us to the house of an old woman who was suffering because her husband had died. We no longer worked with links. Dolster just said her name and asked us to visualize her. When I did, I appeared in a wooden cabin. It was snowing outside, and the old woman lay in her bed. Tears dripped down her cheeks, and her husband lay right next to her, but she couldn't see him. He was slightly transparent and seemed shocked when we appeared. I got the sense that the man had died but didn't realize that he was dead.

Dolster looked at the dead man, extended his arm, and said, "Do not worry, there is no need to retreat into fear. We have come to help you. Your wife cannot see or hear you because you have passed on. Human death is a transition. It does not help you or your wife if you stay here. You must release her and go to the next step of your journey."

The man looked startled, but a new and gentle expression of acceptance began appearing in his eyes. "Yes," he said. "I remember now. I have done this before."

"Yes," Dolster said. "We have all done this many times, but depending on the beliefs we hold during our physical lives, sometimes it is harder than other times to remember that we are transitioning. Let us do a little ceremony together. Would you allow us to dance?"

"Dance?"

"Yes, dance. We could help you say goodbye to your wife."

"She does not hear me, I have tried."

"She does not hear you because you are not speaking with the part of you that is within her."

Dolster's face became blurry. His eyes remained clear and focused, but the rest of his face looked like a double-exposed photograph. Then Umbumi's face filtered through. As Umbumi, he began singing in a foreign language. The dead man opened his mouth in shock, but then he smiled.

I heard millions of voices doubling Umbumi's chant. I felt the ancestors all around us. Umbumi moved his hands in a rhythmic pattern, and I heard the drumming of the ancestor tree. I couldn't resist, and I joined in. I didn't know what I was saying, but the words came to me. My nonphysical body began moving to the beat, and the dead man's smile widened. He said, "Oh, I have been one of you. Oh, I am one of you."

He began dancing and singing. He too knew the words to Umbumi's song. Gradually, the dead man's shape transformed. First, a purple light illuminated his chest, and then it stretched through his whole body, until he was shining brightly like a purple flame.

The old woman on the bed turned towards us, looked directly at the purple flame, and said with a wild look in her eyes, "Bobby, is that you?"

The flame became a glowing orb and moved towards the old woman. It expanded and surrounded her. Her eyes moved rapidly as she spoke softly, seemingly to herself.

Umbumi moved his hand slowly in front of his body and glanced at each one of us. "Let us go back. He has remembered who he is, and he probably wants to talk to his wife in private before he goes home."

This was one of the stranger things Dolster/ Umbumi did with us. Usually, we helped people who were still in a body, especially ones who had begun to reinvent themselves.

Dolster gave several lectures on that subject. He said that consciousness creates neural patterns that it constantly modifies. During one class, he said, "Souls build neural circuits in brains like masons build brick walls, but imagine a stonemason who constantly modifies the house he lives in. Sometimes he might have to take down an entire wall or a pillar. But what about the roof? He needs to make sure it doesn't fall on his head, so he uses wood scaffolding as a temporary support. We can be this temporary support when a being is in the process of creating major changes to their neural networks. We go and hold a vibration for the being. We sing their song until they can sing it. We give them a hand so they can reinvent themselves."

I spent many nights with my teacher singing songs for others. Sometimes intergalactic beings joined us, but we never called them aliens. The word implied that they did not belong to us, but the opposite was true. Even the weirdest-looking creatures could relate to the human struggle and wanted to help. Shape and form didn't matter, because we never confused a being with the vessel they occupied or used to occupy.

One night, Dolster suggested that we go sing a song for Dr. Rab. He wasn't sure whether he should be Umbumi or Dolster, and he kept flickering back and forth, often staying in a state of facelessness for extended periods of time. But it didn't feel impersonal. No matter which face he wore, he was my teacher.

We were in the classroom when he said, "Dr. Rab has begun to restructure himself. He is waking up, but he still has a lot of energy invested in his old self. PsyOp has sent agents to reinforce his fears and keep the neural structures of his old self in place. But Dr. Rab wants to rebuild himself. He wants to tear down the walls that have imprisoned him in the doctrine of materialism and the illusion of separation. Dr. Rab is ready to get to know the larger reality, but he needs a little help. Let's go sing his song."

My teacher gestured to the class. "Close your eyes. Visualize Dr. Rab, or focus on his name with the intention of visiting him."

I felt a sweeping sensation as the outlines of the classroom disappeared. I was floating in midair and looking down at Dr. Rab, who sat on an old red couch, flipping through the pages of a magazine.

His hair was greasy, and his eyes moved rapidly as he turned the pages. A slightly transparent focus aligner was attached to his forehead, and three dark agents attended the machine. My arrival startled them, as did the appearance of the other students shortly after me. I was surprised as well; the other students had all shed their physical forms and were now brightly glowing balls of light.

One of the orbs materialized as Dolster. He looked at the dark agents, moved his hands in gentle arcs, and said, "My dear students, I never told you that I love you."

As Dolster spoke the words *I love you,* there was a loud pop, and the agents disappeared. I assumed that their networks had crashed again. Dolster looked at us with sadness in his eyes and said, "That was my class from a couple of years ago." But then he smiled and transformed into Umbumi.

Dr. Rab still sat on the couch, completely oblivious to us, but as soon as the dark agents had disappeared, he seemed more at ease. He took a deep breath and leaned back.

Umbumi instructed, "Visualize Dr. Rab as a glowing ball of light, filled with joy and happiness. Then begin to sing or dance. Just let that vision find an expression through you. Put your passion into Dr. Rab's beautiful future, and imagine the most beautiful version of Dr. Rab."

Umbumi began to sing. His face became blurry, and I could see trees and plants growing out of his head. He became the entrance to another realm. His human form had completely dissolved, and where he had been standing was now an opening to the jungle. Trees and vines grew through this opening and moved to the familiar sounds of the ancestor tree. The sounds were irresistible. They made me want to dance and laugh at the same time.

While this joy flowed through me, I looked at Dr. Rab and thought that he could easily be wearing a necklace of flowers. I imagined him dancing to the beat and wearing an orange-blossom necklace. I envisioned him holding my hand and singing with me. Tribal melodies played through me. The whole living room was filled with patches of luminous plants emitting a gentle glow.

Dr. Rab put down the magazine and closed his eyes. A broad smile spread across his face, and I heard his thoughts. He wondered why he felt so good, but he didn't go into a thorough analysis of the feeling. His thoughts seemed to dissolve, and I could feel his essence coming to the surface.

A white cord grew out of his chest, and like a tree spreading its roots, it branched out and merged with each of the glowing orbs. Dr. Rab slowly moved his head, and I could feel him resonate in recognition of us. "Yes, I know I am one with you all."

It felt like a nonverbal agreement, a recognition of the truth of love, an alignment of his Akalele. The plants gradually receded and Umbumi reemerged. There was a slight smile on his face, and his dark skin glowed with contentment and wisdom. He announced, "Dr. Rab's Akalele gives us permission to guide him."

One by one, the glowing orbs disappeared, and I felt a pulling sensation guide me back to the classroom. My teacher stood there with folded hands. He nodded and said, "Dr. Rab has joined the new networks, but he needs several more experiences to become conscious of the shift. His Akalele is aligned, but the neural connections in his brain cannot yet support his new level of awareness. His physical self will need to catch up with the agreements his Akalele has made. His personality cannot yet make sense of the larger reality, but there is an opportunity to introduce him to his new path.

"In one of his past lives, Dr. Rab was a slave in Jamaica. He will soon be going to a pharmaceutical conference on a private beach in Jamaica. Ironically, it is the same beach on which he was executed hundreds of years ago. We might be able to help him reconnect with this memory. This will startle his physical self, but also awaken his curiosity, which he can then use to restructure himself.

"He owns a few helpful books that could potentially provide him with an intellectual model to understand his experience. If we successfully reconnect him with the memory of his slave life, he will most likely pick up a book by Carl Jung and use it to make sense of the experience from a psychological perspective. Carl Jung's theory of the collective unconscious is close enough, and it will be a good stepping stone for him to understand nonphysical consciousness and the networks or virtual realities it creates."

CHAPTER 21

That weekend, our teacher brought us to Jamaica. We were a group of six disembodied beings, shifting in and out of the visual representations of the corporeal forms we used to be identified with, but we knew that we were more than the masks we used to wear. We weren't identified with form. We did not have to take a plane or a boat. Our teacher simply told us to focus on Dr. Rab with the intention of visiting him.

We landed on a beach lined with tall coconut palm trees. In the distance rose tall hills covered in lush forests. I saw Dr. Rab walking along the beach with his feet in the surf. He wore gray shorts and a white T-shirt, and he stared into the distance as if in contemplation.

Umbumi said, "We need to hold an energy field for him and then ask him to remember the life he lived here. We cannot decide for him. In the vibration of love, the will of every being must be respected. But we can hold a strong field around him and assist him in reconnecting with his eternal identity. Let's form a circle around Dr. Rab and sing one tone in unison while focusing on this intention."

The other students were still glowing orbs, and as they began to surround Dr. Rab, thin streaks of white light connected us all. I must have been a white orb as well, but I could not see any part of myself. Umbumi began singing, and we joined him. Dr. Rab was still walking, and we floated around him as we sang a single tone into his ears.

The sound surrounded him and eased his thoughts until his mind grew quiet and alert. In this state, he was suddenly able to retrieve the memory of his slave life.

I witnessed the entire episode as if I were in Dr. Rab's mind. The memory washed over him like a tsunami and immersed him in the horrific pain of his past. I was there with him, experiencing his dreadful emotions as we went through it together.

His masters had tortured him for months, and the view of the execution site provided an ironic sense of relief. As a slave, he wasn't suicidal, but the amount of pain he had to tolerate was breaking his soul. He was a first-generation slave, and, because his masters were European, they insisted that all the people they imported must convert to Christianity.

Dr. Rab's slave self knew that the European god was beyond anything his masters could teach him. He also knew that the god his tribe in Africa used to worship was only a simplification of the supernatural. But now his owners demanded that he believe every word in the Bible and renounce all tribal customs.

Dr. Rab resisted. He wanted to keep the customs of his tribe intact and initiate the younger slaves. He was fortunate enough to have been initiated before he was captured, and he wanted to pass on his traditions to the next generation of slaves.

He led a slave rebellion. They still worked for their owners, but they demanded religious freedom. This infuriated his masters, who were afraid of their slaves' mental freedom. They finally decided to execute Dr. Rab as an attempt to end the rebellion.

Now Dr. Rab's gaze was fixed on the hill that was once covered in his blood. I still floated next to him, singing a single tone. I could see and feel his memories. Although the images were gruesome, we were vibrating in complete harmony with his Akalele, in complete harmony with the understanding of his soul's lessons. This harmony allowed him to experience the memories without cognitive dissonance. He didn't have to think about them yet. We were holding a thoughtless space for him.

He remembered how, after his head had been chopped off, he had floated out of his body. We relived this memory together, and it was as though I could see through his eyes. He looked down at the blood gushing from his neck, saw his head roll down the hill, but his fear was gone. He was overcome by the acceptance and peace of nonphysical existence.

He saw a small dot of white light next to him. It pulled him until he found himself traveling through a tunnel. The tunnel was dark at first, but then it became very bright. Soon the light was a pulsating mass of energy. He was out of the tunnel, surrounded by white light, but it did not blind him. It filled him with incredible love and understanding.

All at once he understood the purpose of his life as a slave. He remembered why he had chosen to experience such a brutal existence. He wanted to explore the relationships and power struggles that evolved around authority and property. He wanted to strengthen his commitment to the divine, without being consumed by one belief system.

Dr. Rab absorbed these insights, and then he floated into the light. For a moment, he couldn't see anything, but gradually the outlines of the ancestor tree appeared. Sounds emerged next, and Dr. Rab found himself standing in front of Umbumi. Umbumi looked a little different. I knew instantly that this encounter was taking place before Dr. Rab had chosen life as Dr. Rab, and before Umbumi became Dolster.

I saw this scene from above. Dr. Rab was shapeless, a glowing orb, but his essence was there. Umbumi spoke to him in a foreign language, but his intentions were clear. He suggested that they both pick a life on Earth and try to bring the ancestors' wisdom into the mental health industry that would evolve over the centuries to come.

Umbumi said, "Imperialism has killed tribal initiations, and without them, many healers will forget their song. They will trip over their words and fall on their faces until they are locked up in mental hospitals, where they will drown in fear and shame. I feel called upon to enter this pattern and help to resolve it."

Umbumi looked at Dr. Rab, who wasn't Dr. Rab yet, and said, "I would like you to be part of this mission."

Then I heard a loud pop and found myself back in the classroom.

Dolster smiled and looked at us with his calming eyes. He gestured with his hands to imply a conclusion, and then he said, "We selected this life two centuries ago. I met Dr. Rab in medical school and introduced myself as Frederic Dolster. Although I had no recollection of meeting him, I felt a certain attraction to Joseph Rab. I used to call him Joe. We became good friends.

"Each of us had picked a middle-class family, and our eyes had been glossed over with the trauma most families subconsciously pass on to their children. Although we studied psychiatry, we were driven by fears of inadequacy.

"Without admitting it to ourselves, we both liked psychiatry because it made us feel like we were better than others. We liked to see ourselves in the helping position, patting others on the shoulder while prescribing them medications. But once we were hired by Kings County Hospital as psychiatrists, we realized that it wasn't enough. It was boring to listen to insane people saying the same things repeatedly and giving them the same medications over and over again. We never talked about it, but each of us felt a sense of discontentment. We needed more. That was when Dr. Rab started working with pharmaceutical companies and tried to feel better about himself through monetary gain. "Subconsciously, I wanted to deal with the fear of inadequacy in a different way. I wanted to be a pioneer. I realized that my patients were pointing the way. All of them said the same things in different ways. "I began to believe that there was another reality where you could go with your mind. One day, I asked one of my patients how I could go there, and she said, 'Just by wanting to go there.' For weeks this answer confused me, until one night I woke up, but I wasn't in my bed. I was on a beautiful beach.

"Was I awake? Was I dreaming? I pondered this question for a few minutes, and then Jeff appeared. You all know Jeff. He is PsyOp's recruiting agent. He introduced me to PsyOp and the networks.

"Jeff said that I could become the most powerful man in the world if I chose to work for the organization, but it would require that I be diagnosed with a mental illness. At the time, my marriage had fallen apart, my only son had committed suicide, and I had no interest in life. I had considered suicide myself, but working for a secret organization sounded like a much more interesting option. I agreed to take the job.

"Thank you all for being part of my awakening, but believe it or not, I still have a body in the hospital. They put my body into a coma when I left the curriculum behind. They have control over my body, but I'm free as long as I love all parts of myself."

Our class ended, and I landed back in my bed with a few minutes remaining before lunch. I stared at the door as the last thing Dolster said echoed through my mind: "Believe it or not, I still have a body in the hospital."

All of this was new to me. I had no idea that Dr. Rab had met Umbumi at the ancestor tree before they chose their lives on Earth. I had no idea that Dolster/ Umbumi still had a physical form, and that it was in the mental hospital somewhere. The idea of him as a patient blew my mind.

I walked to the cafeteria and ate alone. I was no longer paranoid about my food. There was sauce on my vegetables, but it didn't bother me. In fact, it tasted delicious.

I thought about Adrian while I ate. I wondered what kind of life he had chosen. All at once, I saw an image of a human-like figure that looked like it was covered in a yellow slime. The image made my heart jump, and I twitched slightly.

I looked up, trying to find some way to orient myself. I stared at the cafeteria ceiling until I felt centered again. I was still where I had been sitting, but I knew I had seen Adrian.

The image was loaded with feelings of despair and confusion, but it also filled me with heroic ambition. I got up and returned to my room.

Later that afternoon, a nurse came to get me. She told me that Dr. Rab was waiting for me in his office. I walked along the bright corridor and entered his office. Dr. Rab smiled. "Take a seat," he said.

I sat down across from him, and he looked at the closed door for a second. Then he said quietly, "Greg, I don't know who to talk to. I've experienced something very unusual."

He said that on his last visit to Jamaica, he had a strange experience. Excited and scared, he described his visions of the slave's life and of Dolster. He formulated his sentences carefully, and I could tell that a part of him doubted his own sanity. He kept saying, "I know this sounds crazy . . ."

He was especially startled by his visions of Dolster. He said, "I had a vision that I met my old friend Frederic Dolster before this life. He went crazy a couple of years ago, but in my vision, he had known me many years earlier and wanted to work with me to change the mental health industry. That was why we came here."

His voice had grown thin as he spoke, and his eyes had clouded over with doubt.

I smiled and asked, "Where's Dolster now?"

Dr. Rab looked startled by my question. His big eyes opened even wider, and he asked, "Do you know him?"

I hesitated. I wasn't sure if I should weave a thread through multiple realities, but then I felt the truth escape my lips.

"Yes, I do. He's my teacher in another reality. He and Umbumi are as one."

As I said this, Dr. Rab's jaw dropped. He shifted uncomfortably, as if he were unsure whether to get up and run away or listen to what I had to say. Perhaps he had thought of his visions merely as daydreams, but my knowing Umbumi's name without being told forced him to consider them as reality.

For a while, he said nothing, and I could see that he was dealing with a heavy load of cognitive dissonance. Then I saw a few glowing orbs appear. They began surrounding Dr. Rab and vibrating in unison. He probably couldn't see or hear them, but their vibration seemed to help him. He cleared his throat and suddenly calmed. He said, "Interesting. Very interesting . . ."

For a moment, he looked thoughtful. Then he smiled gently and said, "Dolster is in solitary confinement. They took him away." Suddenly, he became concerned with another thought. "Greg! This changes everything! There's more to life than we could imagine. Carl Jung knew about this kind of stuff. He believed that a collective subconscious stores all events, and an individual can spontaneously tap into information that wasn't created by his own life experiences. Greg, maybe the collective unconscious is more than Carl Jung thought. Maybe it incarnates into different corporeal forms. Maybe you and I are more than individuals."

The orbs still surrounded him. He closed his eyes and took a deep breath. He began speaking softly.

"I see an image. We are like soap bubbles in the sky, and the air that is within us is all around us. When we die, the soap bubble pops, and we are united with the whole sky."

Dr. Rab opened his big eyes and said, "Maybe it's a metaphor. Our ego, our self as the person we believe to be, is the boundary of the soap bubble, but the collective unconscious is within you and all around you."

We talked for a while about things that a normal psychiatrist would have considered completely crazy. But Dr. Rab was no longer a normal psychiatrist; he was initiated.

CHAPTER 22

The next time I left my body and attended Dolster's class, I asked him about his body and if I could help him get out of solitary confinement.

He shook his head and said, "You have to let time run its course. Let time answer your questions." He seemed at peace, so I didn't ask him again.

Over the next few weeks, Dr. Rab and I continued discussing his experiences. He no longer treated me like a patient. He began reducing my medications, and soon I was taking nothing at all. He even apologized for being unable to understand me before his initiation. He said, "I was afraid of so many things, but now I see your gift. Now I see that you are helping me."

He looked at me with a spark of inspiration and said, "When the larger reality is fragmented by fear, its attempts to integrate are perceived as pathological. Perhaps mental illness isn't a condition, but a process— a process for integrating your fears and bringing forth your gifts."

His eyes widened as if he had just found the key to a hidden temple, but then he added thoughtfully, "I hope Frederic finds his gift . . ."

"You mean Dolster?"

"Yes, Frederic Dolster."

"Did you manage to see him?"

"No, I'm not authorized to see him. Another department cares for him."

"Which department?"

"They're called *Psychology Operation*." I didn't say anything, but I thought that they were probably the physical version of PsyOp. I wasn't sure if I should tell Dr. Rab about PsyOp. I didn't know if it would do any good. It felt like we had both escaped their control and talking about them would only attract more attention to us. Maybe I was still a bit afraid, but I decided not to say anything.

That night, I couldn't stop thinking about Dolster. I decided to try to find him. I closed my eyes and said to myself, "I would like to visit Dolster's body."

I heard the popping sound and found myself flying through a kaleidoscope of colors. Then my vision opened up, and I saw a huge field. At the far end of the field stood a tall wall topped by barbed wire. I began gliding towards the wall, but right before I reached it, I felt an electric shock.

I woke up, startled, in my body. I had never experienced anything like that before. Usually, when I left my body, I could glide through any obstacle. I decided to give it another try. I closed my eyes again and said the same thing. "I would like to visit Dolster's body."

I found myself in front of the wall again. I began to glide upwards, but as soon as I was above it, I saw a metallic grid extending horizontally from the wall. The wall curved around in a circle and the metallic grid covered its entire roof.

Underneath the fence were a few small, windowless buildings, and I got the sense that Dolster was in one of them. I tried gliding through the grid, but I received the same electric shock and landed back in my body.

I opened my eyes and stared at the wall. The fluorescent lamp above my bed was humming softly, and I heard footsteps coming to my door. It was a nurse. She carried a plastic tray with a small paper cup on it.

"Here," she said. "You're required to take these medications."

Surprised, I insisted, "No, I'm not. I don't need medications."

She replied in a stern voice, "Yes, you are legally required to take medications." She had a piece of paper with her. She unfolded it and showed it to me. It was some sort of official document that I had apparently signed after attacking the guy in the prison cafeteria.

She said, "You can drink this now, or we can administer your medications intravenously. The choice is yours, but either way, you will be taking these medications."

Intense fear pulsed through my body. I didn't fully understand what was happening. I didn't know how PsyOp was interacting with the hospital administration. Didn't Dr. Rab have any say in this?

I was too startled and frightened to think clearly. The only things I thought about were the two options she had given me.

The nurse continued, "It will be better for your record if you take the medication voluntarily, and let me tell you, straitjackets are not very comfortable." She smiled sarcastically.

I thought about it for a moment and decided to take the paper cup. I drank it in one big gulp. It tasted like artificial grape juice.

In a bitter voice, she said, "Good boy." Then she left the room.

My vision blurred, and the room began to spin. I put my head on the pillow and closed my eyes. I awoke next to Dolster. I was no longer in my body. We both floated in an empty white room.

Dolster said, "They've taken control of your physical body. They must have found out that you remembered everything and were using your skills for a different purpose. They can't really do much about the

171

fact that we, as spirits, are not responding to fear, but they can medicate and drug our bodies and prevent us from bringing the teachings into physical form. You can't do much with the brain if its neurotransmitters are blocked by synthetic chemicals. We must wait and see what happens with PsyOp.

"Do you feel like sticking around here, working on bringing higher consciousness to humanity, or would you rather join Adrian in one of the lower realms? Imagine all realities like the different parts of a tree that has fungus on its leaves and on its roots. If you want to heal the tree, you must focus on the leaves and on the roots. We have beings from the ancestor tree that are bringing healthy vibration to the roots and leaves of this system."

I was still somewhat confused about how all these different realities were related. Dolster sensed my confusion and explained, slowly and clearly, "When you have a cake with many layers, the top layer depends on the stability of the bottom layer. In a human being, the health of the brain depends on the health of the digestive system. We don't live in a closed system—we're part of a larger organism—and this is what we're trying to heal. All of its subsystems need to be repaired.

"If you incarnate into a lower realm and apply your energy there, you will drive a chain reaction that ripples through all layers of reality. The beings that you affect will affect other beings across many multidimensional lifetimes."

I saw an image of Adrian in my mind. He had the slimy yellow body I'd seen in a vision. Although he didn't have many human properties, I still recognized his energy, as if he were wearing an invisible name-tag.

I couldn't make sense of the reality he inhabited. His surroundings weren't very Earth-like, but his feelings were. I sensed his despair. An intense desire to help him surged through my being.

Dolster nodded and continued, "The fear Adrian feels, the fear that humans here feel, the fear that beings from other stars feel, is all the same fear. It's like a dirty ocean. The ocean is dirtier in certain spots, but it's still all one ocean, and contaminated water can travel from one coast to the other.

"You can clean the ocean by letting it run through your body. The way you think and feel either cleans the ocean or pollutes it. If you confront fear with the true understanding of its origin, you liberate it from its justifications. What is left behind is love and gratitude. Fear is love that has forgotten its wholeness. When you go into the dirt and see the beauty in it, you create a crystal, and this crystal is all our treasure.

"The solutions you create within your own experience are added to the field and become available for all beings. The victory of your heart is a victory for all of us. When you find gold, all beings find gold. We are one tree, one ocean, one organism that tries to lift itself out of the mud and reach the stars. It doesn't matter what you do, what matters is how you do it. How you deal with your experience, how you smile at the doubt in your mind, how much you can love the screaming faces that haunt you at night. This is how you shift the evolutionary destiny of all beings. This is how you transform probabilistic energy fields, this is how you build the new networks. Transform fear into love.

"Adrian will have a child very soon, and you could be his offspring. Having your vibration on his plane would help him remember his true self. He has dug himself into a hole. He believes now that death will kill him. Consequently, he is afraid. He has positioned himself as a rebel and tried to confront the dominant power structure. It's the same story all over again. A powerful, fear-based organization has oppressed most of the population.

"The creatures there aren't exactly human beings. They walk on two legs, but they don't breathe oxygen. Their metabolism is similar to that of fungi.

"Their planet used to have oxygen, but another civilization, now extinct, destroyed the atmosphere and most of the biosphere. The organism that is now the dominant species is known as *Crimaltobia Anaprolis*. They have evolved from an organism similar to slime mold. Since the last mass extinction, their complexity has increased rapidly, and in the last ten thousand years, it has become possible for souls on the evolutionary level of human beings to incarnate into this organism.

"Because of this, the organism has become more human-like; human souls carry with them the habits they have accumulated in human form—which don't even come from human beings, but that's another story. The point is that a body will be available for you. It would help Adrian a lot if you came through as his son. Well, there aren't male and female creatures in the way you understand them. Adrian will be both your mother and your father. He will divide and give rise to another version of himself. What do you say? Are you willing to go?"

I was there as an orb, and it was easier to make these decisions as a spirit, or in the form of my pure Akalele. You don't care as much when you're not identifying with physical existence. As an orb, it's easier to understand the vastness of life and the importance of love.

It wasn't a difficult decision. I wanted to help Adrian, even if it meant I had to experience a difficult life. I resonated in agreement, and Dolster lost his shape. We vibrated together as two orbs, and then he morphed into Umbumi and smiled. He said, "Come with me."

The wall opened, and he walked into the jungle. As the intention to walk formed in my mind, I had legs. I followed him and found myself surrounded by big green leaves emanating a loving luminosity. I knew we were back at the ancestor tree. The feeling of the plants was unmistakable. They filled the air with vibrant sounds and smells.

We walked and glided past these encouraging plants and landed in the clearing where I had first met Umbumi. He began stomping his feet and singing a repetitive song. Purple flames erupted beneath his feet, and several figures appeared.

They all had dark skin and wrinkled faces. Some were distinctly female or male, but others were genderless and hardly even looked human.

We formed a circle, and everyone contributed to the dance. The purple flames erupting under our feet flowed into the middle of the circle, where they created one big fire. When the fire was burning hot and bright, Umbumi gestured for me to jump. I ran towards the flames, clenched my fists, and leapt into the fire. I felt a sharp pain, and then the sound of the ancestors' voices dimmed, like a fading echo.

CHAPTER 23

I was in a dark and silent space that seemed to sabotage my mind. Something pulled on my brain, and I felt an uncomfortable sensation of openness. I was flooded with strange feelings that stripped away my sense of self and my ability to remember.

There was nothing to think about. The only thing I noticed was a vast new world of feelings. They were like rivers gushing into an empty valley, quickly filling every crack and crevice inside me. The past was gone. I couldn't remember Umbumi, and I couldn't remember that I had a body in a hospital. I did remember what I had learned through all my different lives, but the knowledge was detached from the stories, detached from the details. I only remembered them in relation to what I was feeling.

When a feeling came into my awareness, even though I didn't know what it meant, I could decide whether I would like to follow it or not. I could take one emotion and slow it down until it became a different energy. I had no other senses yet; I experienced only feelings for what seemed like an eternity.

Gradually, I began perceiving what I came to recognize as Adrian's presence. I met him like rivers converge. There was no handshake, but I understood that this was a different current making its own choices and producing its own feelings.

Sometimes these other feelings pulled me into very dissonant frequencies, and I felt intense resistance to what I was experiencing, but I was learning. A balancing act emerged, and like two people who learn to dance together, we began creating more harmonious feelings without stepping on each other's toes.

This balancing act became familiar, and a wider variety of emotions entered my awareness. At some point, the interaction of our energy currents became so familiar that I recognized them as forms and shapes. I began to see patterns that I had previously only felt. As I interacted with these shapes, I developed a sense of self and other.

The most familiar other was Adrian, or the being that he was in this realm. His shape, color, and texture were the first forms that I could recognize visually. He was yellow and slimy, and even though his shape was somewhat human-like, there were significant differences. For example, *Crimaltobia Anaprolis* seemed to lack bones.

Since they had evolved from something like slime molds, the only thing organizing each organism's shape was the intention field, or soul, that incarnated into it. Therefore, many *Crimaltobia Anaprolis* looked like human beings, while others looked like entirely indescribable creatures. But none of these creatures knew that they were eternal souls having a strange experience.

Even I was utterly entranced by the stimuli of this reality, and I soon became worried for my safety. Fear was a strong energy field here, and everyone accepted it as if it were an immutable law. Beings did recognize love here, but it was rare. While there were little seeds of kindness everywhere, the normal state of being was panic and stress.

Adrian and I moved around a lot. The landscape was three-dimensional, but there were inconsistencies. Sometimes a cave tunnel acted like a shortcut, leading to a faraway destination but allowing you to walk a significantly shorter distance. The caves were made of a material that was red and much softer than rock. A type of crystal grew there. This crystal grew quickly and formed stratified structures that bore something like a fruit.

These fruits were probably made of concentrated minerals. Our species depended on them for physical survival, so the caves were valuable and a source of conflict. The beings in power made sure they controlled who had access to the caves, and since there was no farming, most of the population was in a state of starvation and stress. Everyone had to risk their lives to absorb nutrients. Every night we walked through the crystal forests and searched for food. None of the aboveground crystal plants were edible, so we had to get into the caves.

Their entrances were guarded by the dominant few, or DF. Our language wasn't based on sound, so it is impossible to write about the names things had. We also lacked an advanced scientific understanding of our own nature, but I assumed that we communicated through scent and chemical excretion, and the information exchanged in this manner created feelings and visual perceptions. The DF had a specific chemical signature and that was their name.

We didn't have eyes, mouths, noses, or ears. Each cell perceived all things for itself and submitted that data to a central nervous system. Somehow, we had the ability to include others in our information flow, and through the variety of feelings we shared, we had developed a language.

I didn't exactly think about these things; I didn't have that kind of intellectual capacity. Life as a *Crimaltobia Anaprolis* was based on immediate survival. We needed the crystal fruits at least once a day, and if we didn't get them, we ran out of energy. The cells within our body would separate and head off on their own to look for food. That meant death. We would disintegrate, and the slime that made up our bodies would seep into the cracks of the ground and continue existence as a type of moss.

We communicated about this possibility often because every day the DF threatened to disintegrate us. They had some sort of substance they sprayed on anyone who tried to enter the caves, and it would cause our cells to separate. The entrances to the caves were covered by a thick layer of yellow slime—the remains of those who had tried to enter without permission.

Many Crimaltobians were desperate. Either they starved to death, or they stormed the caves, where the DF would often kill them.

Adrian and I had a plan. We walked deep into the crystal forest and dug into the ground until we discovered buried passages. Sometimes we found new caves, other times we came across caves already occupied by the DF.

Although our reality was very different than what we were used to as human beings, Adrian's desire to undermine social power structures was already flowering. He had formed an underground organization to feed the starving masses.

From a young age, I was by his side. After I learned to navigate this new reality, I helped him dig holes and collect crystal fruits. Then we distributed them to others, which was very dangerous. The DF communicated that it was illegal to own crystal fruits. The fruits grew only in caves, and the DF claimed to own all the caves. We were always afraid to get caught. Consequently, we put out fear.

In the beginning, we didn't know of any metaphysical teachings, and we weren't aware of the power of our minds, but by the time I became an adult, I started challenging Adrian's worldview. I began to communicate that I wanted to live differently. However, he kept sending me the signal that things would never

179

change, that things were the way they had been and would continue to be so.

Although he was a powerful spirit, this life had exhausted him. Spending a lifetime hiding and stealing had gotten to him, and he often seemed to be close to giving up. But I had a different vision.

I had a moment as a young Crimaltobian that changed the course of my life. I was in a cave after our planet had turned away from our star. It was technically night, but since we didn't have eyes to interpret the radiation of our star, it didn't affect our ability to see. Some other type of vibratory interaction allowed us to navigate visually, so, despite the darkness, I was still looking for crystal fruits.

I had already passed several good nuggets up to Adrian, who waited just outside the hole we had dug, when we sensed that members of the DF were approaching. They were in the cave and headed towards me.

Adrian extended his hand to lift me up, but I was fascinated by the amount of fear I felt. For a moment, I didn't believe the fear. It didn't seem necessary to react to it. Instead, I had a new feeling. My cells no longer feared disintegration. My organism went into a state that I now know as complete acceptance.

The fear of death had guided my life. Somehow this became very clear to me. Perhaps the patterns of understanding that I had developed through my training with Umbumi were coming to the surface. This new feeling was a powerful current destroying the mental and emotional structures of fear.

I communicated to Adrian that I would walk towards the DF. He didn't have a way to respond to the chemical impulses I was sending him. My choice was outside of his known spectrum of possibilities.

I walked forward and sensed the approaching enemy, but as they noticed me, they were incapable of reacting. I wasn't sending any signals based on fear. Apparently, the DF needed these signals to navigate and make decisions, and even maintain their form. The absence of fear stunned them to the point where their cells were unable to communicate anymore. The sudden transcendence of fear was analogous to the discontinuation of gravity.

Imagine a city that suddenly lost gravity. Cars and humans would be scattered across the sky. Reality as we know it would stop. This was precisely what happened in the bodies of the DF members. Since their species had no bones, their cells were held in place only because of an energy field. This field was now disrupted, and the effects were dramatic. The three members of the DF began to melt, and after a few seconds, the ground was covered with a thick layer of yellow slime. Adrian appeared behind me, and for a moment he couldn't react either, but then he grabbed me by the arm and dragged me out of the cave.

For years we communicated about this incident. His system was under the impression that something like coincidence was responsible for the DF members' disintegration. But I knew there was more to it. I hadn't managed to experience the absence of fear again since then, but in my mind, it was now a possibility.

When we weren't looking for food, I sought to revisit the state of fearlessness. But I knew I couldn't approach the DF until I had found it.

I tried to walk towards them once, but with every step, I became more afraid. Before they detected me, I chose to hide behind a tall crystal plant.

Adrian and I were in conflict, because he couldn't understand my obsession with something I couldn't communicate. The language of the

Crimaltobians had no terms that expressed internal states of being, so how could I have explained to Adrian that I was looking for a different state of being? It didn't make any sense to him. Then one day I was hit by divine inspiration, or something like it.

We had just feasted on some crystal fruits. We lacked mouths, so we ingested the fruits by holding them against our bodies. Slime would form around the fruit, and its contents were gradually absorbed. Since we didn't have any human reference points, it didn't seem disgusting or strange. Quite the opposite, in fact. The process was gratifying and pleasant. For a moment we even forgot about the intense fear that usually consumed our attention.

During one of our daily nutrient absorption sessions, I realized that Adrian must understand the difference between how we felt while we absorbed nutrients and how we felt when we were looking for food. I instinctively knew that I could use this difference to make "being" a subject. There was no term or information pattern for it, but by sending different signals, I could point towards the variable, which was our state of being. We felt different when we were afraid than when we were content.

Adrian suddenly understood what a state of being was, and this understanding must have acted as a catalyst to bring forth some of the knowledge his soul had accumulated about the subject. We now had an anchor point from which new knowledge or information structures could emerge.

We both had spent so much time learning about each other's being: in the hospital, working as agents; at the ancestor tree, as medicine women; and with the intergalactic light beings. Most importantly, we loved and trusted each other. This love allowed us to surrender to one another's feelings and trust that even the unfamiliar parts of each other were aligned with our collective well-being. He trusted me, and I trusted him.

We sat in this trust and witnessed new feelings beginning to flow through our bodies. The intensity of these feelings changed our minds and even transformed our bodies.

Both of us had a lot of experience with powerful emotions, and our souls recognized the vibrational signature of the transformative process that was taking place. Our Akalele had taken control, and we were no longer in agreement with the fear field we had been born into. As a result, the organization of our cells changed as well.

Adrian walked a few steps, picked up a crystal fruit, and then morphed into a ball of slime. I relaxed fully and perceived that my sense of self had disappeared, and my shape probably had, too. I was dead, but only as long as I remained in this state. Whenever I wanted to stand up, it seemed like all my cells found each other again and formed whatever shape I wanted.

I played around with this for a while. I created all sorts of shapes. I had only to visualize a shape, and all my cells responded to my intention. I became a pyramid, a cube, a pentagon, and other crystal-like shapes. Adrian and I communicated while we experimented with our newfound ability to shapeshift. We were sending each other signals that we had never sent before.

We possessed a deep understanding of each other's being, which allowed us to create a new language. We knew what we felt, and we knew what we were experiencing. When we shared a feeling, we spontaneously sent each other information patterns that represented what we experienced. It was a natural and intuitive process to label the new states of being we were discovering. Like a cell that modifies its own DNA, we were creating a new language.

We were sending each other signals that communicated a realization that mind creates matter, that love facilities growth, that fear creates enslavement and delusion, and that the honest recognition of one's state of being is the first step on the path to liberation. Little did we know that our discovery was a powerful weapon.

We spent many days and nights traveling through the crystal forest, shapeshifting and imitating the forms around us. Then one night, we encountered a few members of the DF in a cave.

When they were within our reach, we began to communicate with them. I sent them a few information structures about love and fear, and when they received my messages their cells separated. They collapsed and became puddles of yellow slime, but this time I saw their spirits hover above their disintegrated bodies. They retained a human shape, but were slightly transparent. I could even see their eyes. One of them looked directly at me, and I could see in his eyes what he was thinking.

"Am I dead?"

I intuitively responded, "You are dead if you want to be dead. You can leave this reality, or you can reorganize your cells."

We were no longer talking in Crimaltobian. We saw each other on another level. The things I had learned were coming back to me quickly, and I felt prepared to guide this soul. I said, "Crimaltobians are unique beings. Their cells never die; it is only the multicellular organization that stops existing. This is why your souls are now floating above a puddle of yellow slime. But the cells in the puddle are still responsive to your soul's belief. If you believe that you are dead, your cells will not come together again, but if you believe that you have the power to bring your cells back together, then you permit them to exist within a new spectrum of possibilities.

"You are the energy field that organizes your cells. If you believe that something is true, you emit the probability waves of a certain spectrum of possibility. If you believe that you are dead, you exclude the possibility that you can resurrect your body. But survival is not the ultimate goal. If you are interested in exploring other realities and other identities, you are free to do so."

All the DF members received the information I sent. I saw in their eyes that they understood these ideas. Some of them collected their cells and resurrected their bodies, while others floated away as spirits. Adrian and I left the cave. The resurrected DF members watched us climb out of our hole.

Adrian and I spent the rest of our lives as Crimaltobians, sharing our new language and teaching others about eternal existence. The DF slowly disintegrated as more and more beings lost their fear of death and learned to speak the language of transcendence. It became common to shapeshift, and death wasn't considered a threat anymore. Many beings bounced and rolled around as yellow balls, leaving behind their cells at will.

At a certain stage of development, it was no longer challenging to be a Crimaltobian, so Adrian and I decided to move on. We allowed our bodies to seep into the ground, and we floated away as spirits. Intuitively, we found our way back to the ancestor tree and met Umbumi there.

He greeted us with a warm smile and said, "You guys whipped up a tornado down there."

The three of us laughed. It felt like I had awakened from a dream. For a moment, I felt drowsy and confused, but then I remembered that I had chosen the Crimaltobian life to let time pass.

CHAPTER 24

Umbumi told us that there was a chance we could get our bodies back. He said, "In a few months, Dr. Rab is going to get transferred, and he might be able to get access to our bodies. In the meantime, do you guys want to try a strange configuration? What if we tried a parallel human reality in which you guys have a dysfunctional marriage, and I come through as your child who reminds you of the teachings?"

The three of us laughed. By this point, I wasn't attached to the melodrama of one specific life or the archetypal relationships it created. I thought it would be hilarious and interesting to try out an entirely different dynamic. Adrian and I had never been lovers before, and we had never had a dysfunctional relationship. I was excited to experience the emotions of relief and gratitude when we would finally remember the teachings through our child.

Then I thought about Joey. Maybe he would also be interested in a role in our new life. But when I pictured Joey, I still saw the same image. He stood on top of a tree, and he had very bright wings. His blue eyes shone. I couldn't engage with whatever experience he was currently having, but I knew that his incarnation circle wasn't over yet.

Umbumi noticed that I was drawing information from elsewhere and said, "Stay with us. We have a lot to do. The reality we could incarnate into is very similar to the Earth you know."

We were still standing in the lush forest of the ancestor tree, but as Umbumi spoke, our surroundings gradually morphed into the walls of a conference room. Umbumi's face also changed, and we found ourselves standing across from Dolster.

He continued, "We'll have you incarnate into two different families that will imprint conflicting beliefs into your minds. That way, when you meet, there will be a lot of friction that will gradually expose the things your parents have passed on to your subconscious minds. But we also need to make sure that you recognize each other and fall in love. We'll hold a vibrational field around you that will bridge the gap between your social conditioning and your true selves. We'll maintain the field of love and help you align your selves through the information patterns of a romantic relationship.

"You'll make sense of your connection through the expectations of your parents. They will want you to get married, and I will come through as your child to try and help you lift your relationship beyond the conditioning you were born into. At least this is the plan. There is a slight chance that the social conditioning your parents pass on to you will override our ability to remember who we are, and the three of us will go into the depths of human suffering. But we have a lot of ancestors who are willing to help us with this life. They too think it is an interesting life path we are trying to explore. Let's meet the whole team and start planning. Follow me."

He turned from us and walked through the wall. We were back in the jungle, moving towards a tree-covered hill with a cluster of tall rocks on top. We floated towards them, and Umbumi stopped before the entrance of a small cave. He gestured for us to follow him inside.

We floated into the cave and saw several beings sitting around a fire. Some looked human, while others had less-distinct forms. The cave was quiet. Its walls were covered in what looked like finger paintings.

There were a lot of circles in different colors with white lines connecting them.

One of the beings signaled that we should take a seat. This being was barely physical, mostly consisting of purple mist, but the mist condensed into the shape of a female human form.

We sat. Umbumi looked at us and said, "This is Armassa. She is my teacher." I recognized her from my time at the ancestor tree.

Armassa said, "Welcome. Our ancestors have used this cave to plan their lives for a very long time." She pointed to the circles on the wall. "These are the maps they have created. Each circle represents a different realm, but these are all very old branches. I hear you want to go to a newer one with more disharmonious family patterns."

"Yes," Umbumi said. "The idea is to explore patterns that would be relevant to our current body. By exploring a different manifestation of social disharmony, we might be able to integrate these patterns and bring the vibrational solution into the Earth realm in which we currently have bodies."

Armassa gazed intently at us. Her facial expression became distinct. She had the look of a warrior in her eyes. She asked Umbumi, "You still want to use the bodies you occupy now?"

"Yes, but they are being medicated and held in a coma. We thought we would explore a different dynamic while we wait for the situation to change."

"How long do you want to be gone, relative to your current life?"

"In about two months the situation could change. We should be back by then."

"Are you trying to live a full life in that time? We might have to create a branch just for that life. Let me show you the options."

189

Armassa closed her eyes, and the purple mist that had defined her figure began dissolving. A thick, purple cloud spread around the fire. It was so dense, I could no longer see Umbumi or Adrian.

I felt a tugging sensation in my chest, and then I could see again. A ring of fog surrounded me. Wherever I looked, the fog parted to reveal different scenarios. It wasn't just a visual experience, though. I could fully inhabit each of the different realities. When I focused on one of them, I got absorbed into it and had a taste of that specific life.

In each life, I was married to Adrian. In some, I was the wife and he was the husband. In other lives it was the opposite.

I saw situations through the eyes of different characters. I could feel their past, their subconscious beliefs, and all the things they had manifested. They all felt similar because, even though they were models of different possible lives, in each one, my consciousness was the organizing principle of my body. But the environment and the DNA of each character was unique and, therefore, differed greatly from other characters. I felt angry in a few of the bodies I tried out, while in others, I felt sad and passive. But the same desperation was present in each of these lives.

We wanted to live a difficult life, and although it felt terrible to try out these simulated lives, I was still set on following through with one of them. There were also very beautiful emotions that I could potentially experience.

In one reality, I gave birth to our child, and when I looked into her eyes, I saw a spark of light that gave me an incredible feeling. It felt like it was worth an entire lifetime of pain just to hold this child and look into her sparkling eyes. I instantly knew that I wanted to try that life. I was a blond woman with freckles, and Adrian was a bearded man with dark skin.

As soon as I made my decision, I felt a pulling sensation and returned to the cave. The fire still burned, and Armassa sat across from me. A few other beings sat beside her with their eyes closed. She looked at me, smiled, and said, "You want to take the emotional path?"

Adrian and Umbumi still had their eyes closed. At some point, Adrian took a deep breath and opened his eyes. Armassa looked at both of us and said, "You have both picked different lives. Let's keep going until we have a match."

The purple fog blurred my vision again, and I was back in the life-selection place. I scrolled through more lives, and each time I chose one, I landed back with Armassa.

It took several tries for the three of us to find a life that we all wanted to experience. We finally agreed on a life in France. In that life, Adrian was going to be my wife, and I was supposed to meet him at a bar.

Armassa went over all the details of the life with us. She pulled her hands apart and suddenly held a moment in her hands. When I looked at it, I could once again feel the personality that I was going to be; it was as if I was living that moment while maintaining the awareness that I was in a cave.

Armassa said, "You see the blue car driving across the street? You will recognize this moment subconsciously, and without knowing why, you will walk into the bar across the street. There you will meet Adrian, who will be Marie. She will be working there, and you will recognize each other."

We went over a few more potential scenarios. One involved my uncle breaking his leg. I would bring him to the hospital, and Adrian would be working there as a receptionist. But these other scenarios were less likely. The strongest possibility was that Adrian, as Marie, would become a bartender, because her father owned a bar.

After we went over all the significant decisions we had to make, we were ready to start that life. Adrian was going to be a little older than me, but Armassa said it didn't matter who jumped into the fire first. She began drumming, and the beings that had sat silently around the fire joined her.

We all started stomping our feet. The fire in the middle of the circle turned purple, and each one of our steps seemed to fuel it. When it was burning bright and high, Armassa looked at us and gestured that it was time to jump.

Umbumi ran towards the fire and jumped in. He was supposed to come as Adrian's child in about twenty years, but I guess the system must have taken the latency into account. Then I ran towards the fire and jumped in. Once again, I went through the disorienting process of being prepared for another life. Time stopped, the sense of self disappeared, and the concept of waiting to become someone else was inconceivable. Instead, I slowly got used to a new world of sensations.

CHAPTER 25

One of my earliest memories was blooming flowers. They were small and yellow, with a sweet fragrance. But these tender childhood memories were soon drowned out by the terrifying presence of my father.

I had forgotten entirely that I had chosen him, that I had picked this life to learn how to deal with violent and dysfunctional patterns. Instead, I was terrified of his rages and began contemplating suicide. By the age of ten, I had been beaten countless times. I had scars on my back, but I was too ashamed to reveal this abuse to anyone. I kept my emotions hidden, and slowly they began eating me from the inside. I felt empty and hollow.

The school I went to was terrible as well. The teachers reinforced the fears my father had beaten into me, and the other kids seemed to enjoy seeing me suffer. By the time I was fifteen, there wasn't a glimpse of hope left, so I decided to jump off a bridge.

It was night. The stars were out, and a cold wind was moving the trees in the distance. I looked down, and I could see cars driving below. I knew that all my pain and suffering would be over as soon as my body slammed into the road.

Without hesitation, I jumped. When my body hit the ground, I heard a loud pop, and I was floating above a puddle of blood. My skull was cracked, and my brains had spilled into the street.

I saw a small ball of white light hovering next to me. It tugged at me, and I followed it. I began traveling through a tunnel. The ball of white light was at the end of it, and as I headed towards it, it grew bigger.

Eventually, I found myself surrounded by white light. A feeling of complete peace and love came over me, and I bathed in the beautiful vibration. Gradually, the knowledge of the purpose of my last life returned. I understood again why I had chosen such a difficult life, and a sense of sadness washed over me.

Adrian and Umbumi were on my mind. As I began thinking about them, the white light seemed to dim, and slowly the walls of the ancestor cave became visible. Then I found myself sitting next to Armassa.

She glowed like a purple flame, and her face looked intense and serious. Without speaking aloud, she explained, "You couldn't digest what you tried to swallow. Then you vomited at the dinner party while you were supposed to deliver a speech. The people who never got to hear your speech are missing your information. The absence of information can lead to confusion."

I saw an image of Marie, the girl Adrian was now. She was already in her early twenties, and she was depressed and sad. I saw an image of her sitting by a river as tears dripped from her chin. She whispered, "I know I will meet him. I know I will meet him."

I understood that I hadn't just ended my own life, I had also interfered with the lives of people I hadn't even met yet. I hadn't fulfilled my purpose.

This sadness transformed into an overwhelming desire to communicate with Marie, to tell her that she would be okay. I felt a pulling in my chest, and then I felt myself enter that vision fully. The walls of the cave had disappeared, and now I saw lily pads floating on the shimmering surface of a calm river. It was dark, and the yellow streetlights reflected off the water.

Marie sat close to the water at the edge of a lawn. She had brown curly hair and wore a white dress. Her face had gentle features, but Adrian's intensity lived in her eyes.

She wiped her face with the back of her hand and looked at her reflection in the water. I floated quietly towards her, and for some reason, I had the feeling that she would be able to see me.

She looked up, startled, and took a quick breath, but she did not scream. Our eyes met. I saw that she trusted me, although she probably didn't know what she was looking at. I didn't know if I appeared to her as a glowing orb or if I had any sort of human form. I wasn't focused on myself. I was fully focused on her.

Her beauty was overwhelming, her tenderness was heartwarming, and her purity radiated brightly. I wanted to embrace her, hold her, and tell her that I loved her. She looked at me questioningly and asked softly, "Who are you?"

I wasn't sure what to say. She wouldn't remember the human form of Greg, and she certainly wouldn't know that I was her soulmate who had killed himself. So how could I answer in terms that she would understand? Without thinking it through, I said, "I am here."

She blinked a few times and continued looking at me with fascination and curiosity. She asked, "What is your name?"

I said, "I am your friend from another dimension, from a parallel universe. You won't understand, but you must know that I love you."

Without looking away, she said, "I love you too."

I heard a loud pop, and I was back in the cave next to Armassa and Umbumi. Umbumi had a disappointed look in his eyes, but he patted me compassionately on the shoulder.

Armassa was laughing. She looked at me with an expression that implied, "A multidimensional love declaration." At least, that was how I perceived it. She continued communicating with me telepathically. "We have to adjust the plan. Time isn't an issue. We can let

195

time pass as is necessary. Right now, our simulation is running faster than the one Marie is in, but we can adjust that as soon as we decide how you want to be part of her life.

"Umbumi had the idea that both of you give Marie information and teach her to become a channel for the wisdom of the ancestor tree. She already trusts you. Gaining the trust of the channel is the most difficult task in a project like this. Umbumi knows how to work with channels, and he will show you."

I heard another loud pop, and I was back with Marie, floating above the lily pads. She was startled for a second. Then she said, "You are back! Are you Jesus? Who is your friend?"

Umbumi floated beside me. He was a glowing orb, but his shape wasn't quite round. The outline of a human form was still recognizable, and his eyes seemed to hold worlds within them. I saw many faces and personalities shine through his eyes, but I didn't know how Marie perceived him.

I said, "No, I am not Jesus. This is my teacher, Umbumi."

"Umbumi?" Marie asked.

"Yes," Umbumi said.

Marie was surprised but not afraid. She stared at us for a long time before asking, "Am I dreaming?"

Umbumi said, "You are really one of us, but now you think that you are Marie." She said nothing, just looked at us blankly. Umbumi continued, "We would like to speak to you more often. There are a lot of things people in your world don't know. We would like to inform them through you. What do you think?"

"Inform them through me? What do you mean?"

"You can hear us, right? Most people cannot hear us and don't know that we exist. We want to expand their understanding of reality through the wisdom we hold."

"Why can I see you when other people can't?"

"Other people are too afraid of losing their minds or losing control. They cannot interact with something that is completely unknown to them. You know us, you recognize us, and therefore you don't fear us. If you want, you could become a channel."

"What would that mean?"

"Right now, you are not in an ordinary state of consciousness. Your sorrow has brought you to a quiet point; you are in a trance. When you are in your waking state of consciousness, you are far from the consciousness we hold, and it would be difficult to meet. For you to become a channel, you must learn to put yourself into a trance, or a state of consciousness that isn't interrupted by your analytical mind."

"How do I learn how to enter a trance?"

"You already know how to do it, you just haven't discovered that part of yourself in the life you are currently living. Give us permission, and we will teach you through the experiences you will have."

"Yes, I give you permission."

"Good. We will talk to you soon."

The river and Marie blurred, and the walls of the ancestor cave reappeared. Armassa still sat by the fire, and her eyes met mine. I felt the warmth and tranquility of an infinitely generous mother. She held a bubble in her hand. In the bubble was a miniature version of the reality we had just experienced.

I could see Marie sitting by the river. She stared into the distance for a while and then got up and walked away.

Armassa folded her hands, and the bubble disappeared. She explained telepathically, "Now we need to let time pass. We need to give Marie the chance to process this experience. Disruptive contacts are very difficult for humans. The intensity of such a contact can make her whole world seem bleak and meaningless. She could become emotionally dependent on this contact, in which case, her life will become utterly unbalanced.

"To prevent this from happening, we need to let her deal with the loss that she will experience when you don't contact her for a long time. She will miss you, then she will get frustrated, maybe even angry, and when she has finally given up, you can contact her again."

Armassa pulled her hands apart and once again held the bubble. I could see Marie lying in her bed. Her brown hair was tossed to the side, and her eyes moved rapidly. The bubble radiated emotions of longing and despair.

Armassa said, "The only thing we can do is let time pass. If you disturb her field again, she will only become more dependent on you. Marie's Akalele doesn't feel at home where she is. She doesn't feel at home in France, in her social environment, or within her self. The beliefs she has inherited from her family have created a personality that seems foreign to her.

"The closeness she experienced when she saw you and Umbumi is something she craves now, but it is also something that could be potentially dangerous. If she gets too close to you without integrating her experiences into her personality, she could lose touch with her reality because she would be craving your presence more than anything in her world. To balance a craving, one needs to accept that one cannot have what one craves. We can only wait while Marie comes to terms with this concept. Unfortunately, this means that she needs to go through a lot of pain. It hurts when you cannot have what you want."

The bubble was filled with movement. Marie became blurry, and so did her surroundings. It looked like a movie playing at an extremely high speed. The image accelerated until there was only a vibrant energy between Armassa's hands.

She folded her hands and smiled. "Five years have passed in Marie's life. Now you can introduce yourself again."

Armassa gestured, and the walls of the cave disappeared. I felt a strong sense of motion and emerged into a new reality. Umbumi and I floated in front of Marie.

She sat at a wooden table, eating a bowl of cereal, in what appeared to be the common room in a dormitory. Her head bent forward, and she used her right hand to shovel cereal into her mouth. She chewed rapidly, and a sense of urgency shown in her eyes. As I settled into the moment and focused on her, I began to read her thoughts. She was worried about being late to class.

She stood and walked right through me. It was clear that she wasn't at all in the right headspace to communicate with a spirit.

I said to Umbumi, "She cannot see us."

He was an amorphous blob, but as soon as I addressed him, I saw his smile and his dark eyes. He replied, "Yes, she has pushed the spirit world away. Let us talk to Armassa."

Soon we sat again with Armassa in the cave. She held the small reality bubble, but as she looked at us, she folded her hands and the bubble disappeared. "It was necessary for Marie to move in the other direction. Be patient. Let us visit her in a dream."

Armassa stood and told us to follow her. We walked deeper into the cave. It was very dark, but I could see Armassa and Umbumi glowing brightly. I couldn't feel the ground, and the only reference points I had were Armassa's and Umbumi's glow, but their light did not reflect off any walls. I wasn't sure if we were still in the cave.

I saw another light in the distance. It sped towards us–or maybe we were moving towards it—and in an instant we were inside a very bright dome.

Thousands of glowing, faceless, human-shaped figures sat in rows. Purple beings floated above them and adjusted things here and there. They swooped down, touched certain individuals, and took off again.

One of the purple beings floated towards us. Armassa lifted her hand in greeting, and the being returned the gesture. Like the others, it was faceless and human-shaped, but I could still see its eyes through the purple glow.

It looked at us and said, "You are trying to visit your friend in a dream?"

Armassa said, "Yes."

"Follow me."

We flew rapidly over many rows of the glowing human forms before slowing down. Then we neared one particular human form, and the purple being said, "Here is Marie. We are currently trying to help her deal with the stress she is experiencing in school. Right now, she is dreaming that she is failing a class. Although this is a stressful dream, it allows her to experience the cause of the stress: her inability to accept failures.

"We give her as many failure dreams as possible to help her revisit her conditioning. She still does not know who she is, nor the fact that she has an intrinsic worth independent of how others evaluate her. We are trying to help her get through this pattern.

"I know what your relationship with her is, and it will probably be good for her to reconnect with you. Recognizing your unconditional love and your multidimensional relationship could help Marie get over her desire to impress other human beings. Getting to know the larger reality puts human problems into perspective."

Armassa nodded in agreement, and the purple being said, "Go ahead and enter her dream."

It held a bubble between its hands, and in the bubble was a wooden door in a red brick wall. The purple being said, "Enter this door."

As soon as I contemplated how I might enter the door, I was sucked in and found myself in a school hallway.

Umbumi floated next to me. He smiled like always but said nothing. Then a classroom door opened, and Marie ran out. Her curly hair was a mess and tears ran down her cheeks.

When our eyes met, she stopped in her tracks. Her mouth hung open, and her eyes looked back and forth at me and Umbumi. She said, "I know you."

"Yes," Umbumi and I said together. Umbumi continued, "Why do you believe this?" He pointed to everything surrounding us.

Marie looked confused. Then she said, "Am I dreaming?"

Umbumi said, "Yes, all of this is a dream. Look." He brushed his hand along a wall, and plants began replacing the concrete. It wasn't just a two-dimensional pattern; the plants created an entrance into the jungle.

Umbumi took a few steps into the forest and said, "Come, let me show you a place you might recognize."

Marie looked like she had already forgotten whatever was troubling her earlier. She seemed excited and followed him eagerly.

The three of us glided through the jungle. Marie was laughing joyfully. She said, "I don't even have to walk; the air carries me. And the music, the drums, I recognize them."

We reached the clearing and continued up the hill towards the big rocks. We stopped at the entrance to the cave.

Umbumi said, "This is where you decided to become Marie. Do you remember?"

Marie's face blurred, and I saw Adrian's smile behind her lips.

"Yes," she said in a deep voice. "I was Adrian. I remember now." Her face dissolved, and she became a glowing orb.

At that moment, I felt a strong pull. My surroundings became indistinct, and soon I was back in the giant dome, the dream school. The purple being, Armassa, and Umbumi were there too.

The glowing figure that had been asleep before now stood. The purple being looked at us and said, slightly surprised, "You woke her, but her body is still asleep."

Umbumi said, "Her Akalele knows how to be awake outside of the body."

The glowing figure took on the shape of Adrian and said, "I remember who I am. Thank you all."

His words rippled through us and sent shivers of love and gratitude through my field of awareness. Adrian was back. He was there without fears or worries. We communicated telepathically. It was as if invisible wires allowed us to share our thoughts at maximum efficiency, and they synchronized the four of us. We discussed how to proceed.

It was clear that Adrian was done with the dream school. He could no longer believe himself to be a girl who needed to please her teachers, but he still wanted to finish Marie's life.

We talked about the difficulties he would face. Although he was able to transcend dream realities, the nervous system of a physical body was a different story. He would still wake up and believe himself to be Marie. He knew that he wasn't going to be able to integrate the full awareness of his Akalele, at least not immediately, but he was willing to go through the slow process of awakening in physical form.

We were unsure whether Marie's body would be able to remember this dream. How would she make sense of an awakening that surpassed her entire life? How would she make sense of the concepts of formless awareness, the ancestor tree, multiple bodies, and all these far-out experiences?

We considered the possibility that Marie might go insane. We used that word carefully. When the purple being brought up the topic, it specified that it was talking about losing the balance between physical life and nonphysical experiences. It shared with us a probable future in the form of a reality bubble. In the bubble, we could see Marie in a psych ward. Her parents sat next to her while she communicated with all sorts of spirits.

The purple being explained that once Marie opened the door to us, she would also have the ability to communicate with any being in the nonphysical reality, including agents of PsyOp. But Adrian wasn't afraid of that possibility; he trusted that his experience as Adrian had taught him enough to reject the temptations of the dark side.

He was sure that he would find his way out of the psych ward and turn down offers based on fear and the desire for power. It was a sensitive topic, because there was still a statistical chance that the project could fail, and Marie would end up being medicated for the rest of her life.

We wanted to help Marie lift her personality to the vibrational level of her Akalele and help her share the wisdom of the ancestor tree. Adrian's adventurous spirit came through. He told us not to put too much emphasis on safety. He said, "Let's open her mind all the way."

The next morning, Umbumi and I floated above Marie and watched her awaken. There was something wrong with her eyes. One of them seemed to be looking right while the other looked left. She blinked frantically, and her face twitched.

Umbumi looked at me with urgency and told me to follow him. The wall to Marie's left transformed into a lush forest. We floated into the woods, and Umbumi said, "Her left and right hemispheres aren't synchronized. The high variation of her Akalele is coming into her physical form too quickly. We will need to get help immediately." He flew straight up, and I followed him.

We passed the treetops and entered a low-hanging cloud. Umbumi said, "Repeat these words: Complex B supernova space trone."

I did, and as I finished, I felt an incredible energy shoot through my field of awareness. My vision blurred, and I found myself in a vast space of infinite proportions. Everything was cloaked in vibrational strings of different colors. The colors themselves were the vibrations, and I could see, hear, and feel them at the same time. Whatever dimension we entered apparently lived by entirely different rules, or maybe it was such a highly evolved reality that completely new resonance patterns emerged and formed multi-sensual crystal structures.

I didn't know how to process the input that my senses received. Thoughts weren't linear or rational, but I didn't feel uncomfortable. The energy in this space was so strong that I didn't even have a chance to resist or consider my experience from another perspective. We had merged with this reality, and we were vibrating harmoniously with everything in it.

Through this harmonious and pleasant vibration, we began to exchange information with multiple intelligent energies. They were formless, but as they expressed themselves, they took on shapes and colors.

These beings didn't seem to be separate from the multi-sensual language they spoke, wrote, and radiated. They knew why we had come, and they were willing to help us. They told us to go to Marie and hold an energy field of love. They said that they could only reach Marie if we created a strong enough energy field for them to come through. We were to act as some sort of bridge for them.

We rushed back to Marie and saw that only a brief amount of time had passed. She was still in bed. It was Sunday, and she didn't have to go to school, but she didn't look well.

I could see the unconditional love of Adrian's Akalele clashing with Marie's personality. Her eyes still twitched, and she flickered between frequencies. First fear would rush through her whole body, and then she would smile, even laugh a little, before collapsing back into lower vibrations. She was unable to ground the power that was flowing through her brain.

She noticed us. She said a few unintelligible words, but then looked away, distracted by other thoughts.

Umbumi looked at me and said, "Don't worry, just radiate love. Put your hands next to her and feel the ancestor tree, feel the flowers. Send Marie good wishes and stay focused on that energy."

I focused on love and peace and wished Marie to feel that too. I stayed focused on that intention, and an intense tingling traveled through my nonphysical hands. A white glow spread around Marie. She closed her eyes and took a deep breath. The bright circle extending beyond her body.

In the middle of the circle, I saw a spinning light. The light was golden and grew into a vortex. Then it dipped down like the tip of a tornado. The tip was small but seemed powerful and focused. It moved up and down her body and stopped right between her eyes.

When the energy vortex touched Marie's head, her entire body jolted, but she didn't open her eyes. The vortex began engraving intricate patterns into Marie's body, restructuring the flow of energy within her.

Whenever the tip of the vortex moved away from a spot, it left behind a glowing thread. The threads outlined geometric structures that looked like crystal or snowflake patterns. Umbumi and I still floated next to her, focused on holding a field of love.

The vortex worked on her forehead for a long time. Then it moved down to her heart and began creating patterns there. Next, it moved up and down her neck, connecting the patterns on her head with those in her heart. This went on for a while with slight variations. Sometimes the vortex took on different forms as it engaged with various parts of Marie's energy field.

Since we didn't have physical bodies, we didn't get tired, but it seemed to be very exhausting for Marie. Sometimes she left her room to go to the bathroom or to drink some water, but she could barely walk. She stumbled through the living room and returned to her bed as soon as she could.

Towards evening, her roommate, Annabelle, came home. She called Marie's name, and when Marie didn't answer, she walked into the room.

"Marie," she said. "What is going on with you?" Marie opened her eyes slowly and said, "Aliens are abducting me." Annabelle's eyes almost fell out of her skull. She knew Marie wasn't joking, but Annabelle didn't believe in things like that.

Annabelle's mouth was open and she made gasping sounds. Her thoughts raced, and I could feel a ripple of fear disturbing our field. Annabelle had intense energy, and her worries interfered with the field we were holding.

The white circle surrounding Marie disappeared, and she sat up abruptly. Annabelle's fear had reached her, and Marie began screaming at the top of her lungs. Annabelle slammed the door, and I heard rapid footsteps echoing through the living room. Then I listened to the sound of the front door opening and closing. I assumed that she had run away to get help.

Umbumi and I remained next to Marie and focused on recreating the love field, but we couldn't get Marie to sync with our vibrations. She was off in her thoughts, being tossed in circles by the fear her roommate had projected onto her.

Her rational brain had tried to make sense of the procedure and had decided that she was being abducted by aliens, but she grew up in a social environment in which aliens, nonphysical beings, or spirits were unacceptable. Those were things insane people talked about, which was why she responded to the worries of her roommate.

At the same time, her Akalele wanted to come forth and express itself to her full potential. This

207

conflict destabilized Marie. She lay in bed, twitching, with her eyes rolled upwards. There wasn't much Umbumi or I could do at this point. We sent her love while we waited to see where this situation might go.

After a few hours, Marie's parents arrived, which, of course, made everything much worse. They were seriously concerned, but they had no idea how to help a being align with their Akalele. They just piled their worries and fears on top of Marie's already destabilized field, and she collapsed even further.

They called an ambulance, and she was brought to a hospital. After an examination, she was taken to the psych ward. Adrian now had two bodies in mental hospitals.

We sat invisibly next to Marie and tried our best to help her re-enter the spectrum of love. But the worries of her social environment had trapped her in the lower vibrations, where the agents of PsyOp awaited her.

I could see them swirling around her like vultures circling above a dying animal. They started sending thoughts that would engage her ego. They tried to get her to enter into some sort of agreement. But Marie was unresponsive. Deep down, she recognized them, and she wasn't going to make the same mistake twice.

She lay in a white bed, and her eyes were closed, but I could feel what was going on inside her. To my surprise, the agents gave her some sort of orientation. She recognized their energy, and when you recognize down, you also recognize up. As she hit rock bottom, her energy began climbing again.

Eventually, we could reach her, and she began resonating with our field. Umbumi and I focused all our energy on holding a stable field of love.

The white circle surrounded her body again, and suddenly the golden vortex reappeared. With extreme precision, it resumed drawing patterns upon her body. Then the golden vortex transmitted images to Marie. I could see them floating around her head.

Each picture had a thought or realization attached to it, which addressed the false beliefs with which Marie agreed. It isolated them and exposed the assumptions upon which they were based.

She saw her parents' concerns from a different perspective, and she realized that she didn't need to agree with their fears just because they had raised her. She didn't need to be in agreement with the fear of aliens or nonphysical beings just because others were afraid of the unknown.

She began trusting her experience and fully received the love we sent her. A smile formed on her face, and she began breathing deeply and slowly.

We allowed her to soak up this vibration for as long as possible, and within a few days, Marie was a different person. The doctors were surprised by her rapid recovery, and they told her parents that they didn't know why or how she had bounced back so quickly.

Marie became a radiant woman. She knew who she was but no longer felt the need to explain it to anyone. Later, when someone would ask her about her mental breakdown, she would reply, "The darkest experiences can show you the light that has always been present."

Marie could see and hear us without losing balance. She understood that here and now was the place she would always be, no matter what other experiences she would have.

She finished school and got a degree in psychology. She wrote books on mental illness and dealing with experiences that surpass the rational mind.

Her wisdom attracted many people, and she began lecturing and holding workshops. She helped create a community that allowed mental patients to go through their transformational journeys outside the limited mindset of conventional psychology.

Umbumi and I were there with her the whole time. She chose to keep her channeling capabilities to herself, but much of the wisdom Marie put into her books came from us. When she was asked where her ideas came from, she said, "Wisdom speaks for itself."

Marie spent the rest of her life in a small house in the French Alps. She was a happy old woman. One night, her Akalele decided not to return to her body. Instead, she met us at the ancestor tree.

Armassa, Umbumi, and I were sitting around a fire when a glowing orb appeared. Although it wasn't showing its face, I instantly knew that it was Adrian/Marie. He/she said, "I have decided to move on. Marie has fulfilled her purpose."

Armassa touched her chest and lowered her head. Then she said, "Good. What a beautiful life you lived. Let us continue with Adrian, Greg, and Dolster."

She pulled her hands apart and created a reality bubble. Inside it, I saw a miniature version of a hospital. It looked old and run-down. The walls were cracked, and the windows were broken. I felt the echoes of silent screams. Armassa looked serious and focused, but then she smiled and said, "We have planted many seeds. Now they have sprouted."

When she said this, plants began growing out of the broken windows and cracked walls. The plants had the thick green leaves of the ancestor tree. As they grew, I felt the drumbeat in my heart. Flowers emerged from the tips of several tall plants. Each flower had dozens of radiating petals that glowed white with a purple hue on their fringes. Just when I thought they were done blooming, big white orbs came out of their centers. In the middle of each orb was a face.

One orb had my face on it, another had Adrian's face. I saw Dolster's face, and Dr. Rab's as well. There were dozens of other faces I didn't recognize.

Armassa said, "We have transformed PsyOp from the inside. Our mother's sister is free. The new networks are growing. Water them, serve them, go and sing your song."

My vision blurred, and I found myself floating in a vast space of white light. It was a familiar place, but different than all the form-based realities I had interacted with.

My essence felt completely at peace and, at the same time, intertwined with everything around me. The light was me, but I could perceive the light as separate from me. There was a delicate dance between oneness and separation that felt beautiful and natural.

Within this dance, I began perceiving my parents. They were floating towards me, sending me welcoming thoughts in unison. "Our dear son, we are so proud of you. We have also been on quite a long journey, and we have decided that we want to come back to Earth. We would like to come as your children. Twins. We want to come as twins."

Follow the evolution of this project at
wenzlmcgowen.com